Essondale

David Laing Dawson

Bridgeross Communications
Dundas, Canada

Library and Archives Canada Cataloguing in Publication

Dawson, David Laing
      Essondale / David Laing Dawson

ISBN: 978-0-9810037-4-0

    I. Title

PS8557.A85E8 2009 C813'.54   C2009-900035-0

Cover design by the author

Bridgeross Communications
Dundas, Ontario, Canada

Also by David Laing Dawson

Fiction:

Last Rights

Double Blind

Slide in all Direction

The Intern

Non-fiction:

Schizophrenia in Focus

Relationship Management

Film & Video:

Who Cares

Manic

My Name is Walter James Cross

Painting with Tom, David and Emily

Cutting for Stone

For Erin and Jonathan

ONE

Robert Snow closed his eyes against the sudden light of the setting sun as he stepped out of a tavern on Hastings, and felt his way along the storefronts, walking west toward Chinatown, toward his room on Water Street. He didn't look behind, to the east, where he knew the last pink rays would be capping the coastal range with fictitious warmth. He kept his head bent to the sidewalk, his eyes on the papers and dirt in the gutter and at the foot of the buildings. He raised his head just enough to navigate around people and poles, not enough to see their faces. He craved invisibility. Shit-kicking drunk he was, fucking right.

Listing into doorways, leaning toward the walls and plate glass windows as if to counter a force pulling him into the street, tacking against some internal wind, he made slow unsteady progress from one tavern to the next, past dirty variety stores, the Communist Bookstore, still in business, he couldn't fucking believe it, more tenacity than Dr. Robert Snow, Dr. fuck-up Robert Snow. He passed black barbecued, dripping, unidentifiable animals hanging from black metal hooks in small oriental groceries. They reminded him of something. Where he should be. Well, hell, he'd said it. He'd looked it up, Italian and French, and said it to her, Ti amo et Je t'adore. Christ, got the French wrong, but she'd asked him to stay anyway, and a few weeks later he was back on the bottle. Running. Jennifer saying to him, "So, you give me a little test. Show me the shit hopeless side of your personality and whine such a sad do you still love me? Well I got news for you, Robert Snow, the answer is no." And the no hadn't been one of her cute no's, the edges sort of squinched up, it had been a rock hard no as she shoved him out the door. He'd felt relief for a good ten minutes and then that goddamn awful crawling emptiness. Too late.

He paused for a moment beside a new set of swing doors, saloon doors, and then tilted forward, letting his weight carry him the last step to the threshold and through, once more into the cool, hazy, amber comfort. He opened his eyes to this kinder light and eased into a chair along the side, like an old man getting into a tepid bath. His back was protected by a wall, his front by a round and stained terry-clothed table. He was wearing a rubbie's coat. His hands were unsteady and he hid them in the pockets.

The sounds around him were loud and harsh and he could make no sense of them - strings of syllables, expletives, laughing, coughing. He imagined impassioned points being made, dirty jokes told, bonds being forged and broken, but he felt more kinship with the derelict on his left talking with conviction to phantoms above an empty chair, and more affinity with the watchful Indians, the first people, in the corner, their corner, drinking seriously and defiantly, their eyes unreadable.

"So. What'll it be?" A waiter with a full tray was standing over him, a tattooed forearm below his sleeve, impatient for a show of cash, money on the table. Snow fumbled in his pocket for a bill, pushed past a bottle of pills and came up with five dollars.

"Two?"

He nodded and kept his gaze on the table. He was awash with self-pity and knew he was awash with self-pity. He was feeding that monster within, two dialogues running in his head, one justifying what he was doing, the other giving himself shit, and maybe a third laughing at it all. The waiter put two glasses on the table and Snow drank from one. The cold liquid momentarily quelled his nausea, and drew his attention from the pain through his temples, behind his eyes, and he remembered those long wasted afternoons of his underage youth drinking anxiously, then boisterously, with his friends, each following the other's lead, exploring some limitation, until they were thrown out in the late afternoon, their pockets full of beer glasses.

His sickness returned as he shakily replaced the glass on the absorbing cloth, and then, feeling in a non-specific way that any one of his organs might shortly erupt, he pulled himself to his feet and felt his way between the tables and chairs, the grumbling, complaining, afternoon drinkers, his vision fixed on the washroom sign ahead. When he was almost there the huge flickering television screen caught his eye - soaps, commercials, talk shows - he couldn't tell. He tripped on a leg and sprawled across the shoulders of a big man in a plaid shirt. Making rapid apologies he untangled himself and hurried for the washroom door, though for a moment, shit, he wondered if taking a good beating from a drunken unemployed logger might be a reasonable ending for the day, and might prevent the other ending forming in his mind. He steadied himself for a moment just inside the door, squinting against the strict fluorescent light, then shuffled up to a urinal, placed his head against the cold wet pipes, pressed his elbows into the hard stable porcelain, and let out a long breath. He knew that any discharge would relieve some of the pressure in his body but it was slow starting and so he shifted the weight on his feet, inhaled deeply, leaned his head back to better see the graffiti on the wall, and grasped the cool plumbing with his free hand.

Right before him was the usual drawing: sausage legs, tits to the air, small square feet, knees raised, thighs spread, and between them an exotic bush carefully and lovingly rendered with sweeping artistic flourishes. Some of the parts were crudely named and this made him think of Larry Rivers' labelled nudes: vagin, teton, capezzolo. Christ, he was a fucking cultured man having a thought like that. Rivers getting what now? A few hundred thousand for his drawings? And this thing on the wall, crude maybe but charming in its simplicity, a direct visual statement unfettered by irony, allusion, immediately available, easily reproduced, naively ambivalent, as Eddy might put it. Ah, man's relationship with women. All there before him. What's the difference between this and the shit you do, Larry? Fuck. Looking down he found himself pissing on the inside of his coat, down his trouser leg, and across his left shoe. My apologies, Mr. Rivers. He shook himself free. Whores, goddesses, mothers and daughters. Can't live with 'em, can't live without 'em.

Back on the street he flapped his coat open and did a little jig to waft some air up his left leg. He heard pills rattling in their container in his pocket, and listening to their music, made up his mind. The decision calmed him somewhat. It lifted the pressure from his chest, made the sunlight more bearable, and he looked into the faces of his fellow travellers. Dull eyes with tension lines, unhappy mouths, gravity resting heavily on their shoulders. It was what he saw or wanted to see. A block closer to Water Street he came across a lunatic dancing in a winter coat, pointing to the west with a long crooked finger, tapping out a rhythm with his feet, eyes intensely focused, preaching someone's truth or vision.

He passed by, walking in the direction the man was pointing, to the west, into the setting sun. Maybe he should listen to the ocean for a while, or gulls squawking shamelessly over a garbage barge, or maybe write a note explaining. So look Jen, he'd told her, you don't need me, I'll get into a serious depression, it's in the family. Yeah, so, you get depressed you take antidepressants. Just like that? Yeah, just like that. It's treatable for Christ's sake. She made it sound all so possible, him moving in with her and the two kids, even if he didn't get his licence back, and his daughter saying he was fucking hopeless, and his wife back in Toronto living in their big overpriced home with him still paying the mortgage. Guilt money.

At a liquor store he bought a bottle of Control Board Scotch and stuffed it in his pocket before making his way the final few blocks to his hotel on Water Street, laboriously climbing three flights of stairs and entering his room exhausted. He placed the scotch on the bedside table, then the bottle of pills, took off his coat, laid it across the chair, sat on the bed and examined the simplicity of his refuge. The brown-green wallpaper had little figures on it doing something, he couldn't tell what, their actions lost in the overall pattern, jumping, squatting, fornicating, dancing, carrying lanterns or buckets. Carrying buckets. Why would anyone design a wallpaper of little people carrying buckets? A breeze fluttered the ragged curtain by his window, and the thought of sitting by this window one more Sunday, calling Jennifer long distance from the phone down the hall, getting no answer, and then calling collect and hearing her refuse the call, and then getting through but having her hang up, then walking aimlessly, coming back, sitting, staring into the street below, his mind numbed by flaccid indecision, without point or purpose...Ah, shit. He began to drink directly from the bottle, changed his mind, retrieved a glass from the top of the bureau, and filled it with whiskey. He took the pills from the bedside table and settled into the cushioned chair by the window. So he was going to actually do it. Amazing. He'd watched himself get to this point before, but never beyond. He watched himself now, as if detached, separated from his body, watching this person, this washed up, rejected, failed, Christ, what bathos - self-pitying, wretched, asshole, just sitting there doing it, not to get attention, what had Willy Loman's wife said, pay attention to this man? Attention must be paid? Not so cultured after all. No. Just take himself out of their lives. A fully rational decision. Or make one shit of a mess trying.

They brought him on a Gurney in four point leathers. His ankles and wrists were each cuffed in padded dog collars and lashed to the metal frame of the Gurney.

Marjorie Brennan knew why she hated being on call. At the worst moments they'd bring in a psychotic or a drunk or a drunk psychotic, just when she'd settled in for the evening, given up all ideas of adventure and settled into something mind-numbing on the tube. Now her Sunday last month was something else. He'd come by, she wasn't up to naming him, even to herself, he'd come by, and she'd taken him to the small duty room, and then, well, Christ, she'd been so ambivalent and he'd been so nervous it was very inconclusive lovemaking. She hadn't come. He'd commented on it, and she'd told him it was just as well, because when she came she came like a bomb. Well, it used to be true.

She sat at the desk in the small examining room and looked over the sparse notes from the jail. She'd left the T.V. on in the duty room, the beginnings of some late night movie.

She guessed he was here now, not earlier in the sensible daylight hours, because the ward doctors had stalled all afternoon. The note indicated an overdose of alcohol and barbiturates, cleared at the general hospital emergency, that he spent last night in jail, went crazy sometime today, was given a big dose of Haldol and shipped out. The note started calling this man John Doe from a seedy hotel by the inner harbour but ended with the last name, Snow.

She glanced up at the two aides waiting by the gurney. She got up, said, for something to say, "They thought he was going psychotic and gave him ten Haldol I.M." She looked down at her new patient.

"Mr. Snow?" she said, "I'm Dr. Brennan. Mr. Snow. Are you awake?"

The man didn't respond.

She examined him quickly, pulling back his eyelids, flashing a light on his pupils, pulling his lip down, feeling his carotid pulses, listening to his chest, pushing under his rib cage to find a liver. His breathing was loud and dry. He smelled of old vomit and dirty socks but he didn't have the face or body of a veteran of the alleys. He was new to this.

"Maybe we could take his straps off?"

The male aide said, "Might be wise to leave them on."

She looked at the aide. "He's out of it. He can't keep his eyes open." To demonstrate she gave Snow a hard squeeze on the bridge of his nose. His eyelids flickered and he cried out. He briefly raised his head and then let it fall back. His eyes opened and focused on her. He moved his hands.

"I'm tied down."

"You gave them a pretty hard time at the jail."

"Don' remember." His eyes closed.

"Do you know your name?"

"Hmmmm."

"Do you know where you are?"

"Here. Somewhere here."

"What city then? Let's start with that."

"Vancouver. Toron'o. Wha' diff'rence..."

She asked, "This place then? This building. What is it?"

"Hospi'al. Prob'ly a fugging looney bin." He looked at her again but his eyes faded and lost focus. He smiled slightly and began to mutter. His muttering was incoherent. Fear and humor alternated on his face. He struggled to free his hands, then moaned and arched his back.

She let the aides wheel him away and sat down to write her admission note and orders. Male Caucasian, approx. 45, no fixed address, delirium, presumed alcohol and Haldol intoxication. Adequately hydrated. No apparent infection. No apparent head injury. She ordered seclusion, mattress on the floor, q 15 minutes observation, blood work, skull XRAY, Cogentin IM, 2 mg. stat, push fluids, thiamine 100 mg. IM, B vitamins, filled out forms 36 and 44, stretched her long legs under the table, glanced at her watch. It was too late to call home. She really should go around to the wards and see if the nurses needed anything. Or she could read a journal, or finish that bag of cheesies sitting on the TV in the duty room.

On her way off the ward she stopped to peer into the concave window of the new patient's seclusion room. He was facing away from the door, hospital gown split open at the back. He seemed to be walking slowly and carefully into the corner, squeezing himself in, surrounding himself with walls.

THREE

Awaking alone in the small house on 23rd Melanie listened to the sound of the refrigerator clicking on and off, the birds outside her window, the traffic on Oak Street. She felt young, pampered and safe, luxuriating in the warmth of her bed. Any moment now mother would enter her room and open the curtains. She raised herself on one elbow and looked at her Swatch on the bedside table. She pulled several crumpled sheets of paper from under her pillow, smoothed them out and read her poems aloud. They pleased her immensely. Awesome she thought, totally awesome. I must show these to Dr. Guscott.

She dressed quickly, decided against panties, pulled on designer jeans, and then a cotton shirt with long sleeves to hide the scars on her wrists. She examined herself in the mirror. With her short straight blonde hair she could look pretty and vulnerable or drab and plain and rather butchy. The transformations were startling to her friends and therapists but of no great surprise to Melanie. She knew how fleeting her sense of self could be and how much it depended on the wishes of others.

Today her reflection was sweet and vulnerable. She must go to Dr. Guscott and give her poems to him. She might be coy at first, a little indirect, just hint about the pages in her purse, maybe have them in a peach colored folder, then offer them reluctantly and watch him read, just the two of them, alone in his office, and then... but here the scene faded. Images from movies and television vied for attention in her head, romantic heroines from the past, at once clutching, embracing and rejecting their lovers. Greta Garbo, Jean Harlow. People said she looked like a young Jean Harlow. She struck a languid pose before the mirror. Perhaps she needed a barrette in her hair and a little pink gloss on her lips to make a picture of innocence.

In the kitchen she phoned the hospital and asked for Dr. Guscott. The ward receptionist told her the doctor was busy and would she care to leave her number. Yes she answered and gave her number slowly.

But now the perfect day was spoiled. She made herself some toast, beginning to hear a thrumming in her Silver Thread. Damn. High and mighty Dr. Guscott. He doesn't care. She spread peanut butter on her toast and sat down at the kitchen table. The house was quiet. The fresh morning coastal chill had been replaced by hazy Pacific sunlight. Her eyes drifted to mother's blouses piled beside the iron on the ironing board. Mother had trouble deciding on a blouse each morning although she always wore white - trouble finding a particular design and collar to suit her mood. Would you believe it?

There was something about the blouses that annoyed Melanie. Mother was everywhere - spent teabag draped on the edged of a saucer, list of extension courses pinned to the fridge with a Garfield magnet, Italian sandals under the table, magazines like Omni and Equinox, self improvement books, pantyhose draped over the shower curtains. Poor mother. Doesn't really deserve me screaming at her all the time. But so nosey, wanting to hear everything, every little detail.

Mother's soft plaintive voice echoed in the back of her brain. She phoned the hospital a second time. "It's really urgent," she said, a small tremor in her voice. "I have to talk with Dr. Guscott. Yes, it is urgent." And it became urgent as she spoke. But she was put off once more.

She hung up, waited, picked up the receiver again and dialled Lifeline. "Hello," she said in a very soft voice. "I feel sort of funny. I don't think I can cope any longer."

The voice on the other end was solicitous, deeply sincere, and yes, anxious, a little anxious when Melanie agreed she'd been thinking of taking her life, with pills maybe, and she is seeing somebody but he won't return her calls, Dr. Guscott at the hospital, six, two..., but I guess you know the number. She let her voice trail off before hanging up. She sat tapping her fingers on the telephone for a minute and then dialled the hospital again. I'm sorry said the receptionist, Dr. Guscott isn't answering his page.

So she had no choice. Even Dr. Guscott had deserted her. She took two bottles of pills from the bathroom medicine cabinet, returned to the kitchen, poured a glass of water, sat at the table, and began to swallow the tablets one at a time, playing with each, spreading them and counting, one eye on the telephone, Elavil, Valium, sacraments to her love for Dr. Guscott, who would answer her calls if he really cared.

The yellow Elavil tablets belonged to mother who has been taking them for simply eons. They conveyed the same distasteful intimacy as a wet toothbrush. She gagged a little, continued, beginning to understand that she had stepped into something, once more crossed a line.

Melanie swallowed the last two tablets, one yellow, one white, and listened to the tightening of her Silver Thread. The telephone refused to ring and the back half of her mind engulfed the front half threatening to make her blind. Mother's voice began to stir in the dark half of her mind, in the cave of its permanent home.

"I tried my best after all. Wasn't I the one to stand by you after that terrible thing happened?"

"It was rape, mother, rape."

"All right then, rape, if you must say it. You have to understand. It's been lonely trying to raise two girls without a father. It's been difficult for all of us. I didn't know what your father would become when I married him. I should have left sooner, taken you and Carol."

"Stop it. Just stop it. You have no right to talk to me like that." Melanie couldn't remember what she had said that was so hurtful. Something to wipe the soft smile off mother's face. And then Annie, mother - her best friend, best friends don't have to say mother - Annie would get that hurt look on her face, and Melanie would feel like shit, just like shit, but she'd keep at it until...

It was getting fuzzy, confusing, and Christ did she ever feel sick. She staggered from the kitchen to the bathroom, steadied herself on the sink and looked into the mirror. The reflection refused to stay still. Her hair looked dirty. Mother's face rushed out to greet her with its worried blue eyes, bittersweet mouth. She'd be wearing her frilly blouse, her puffy cravat, her knee length skirt, maybe her pink choker, Spanish comb in her white hair, everything so cute and sugary it made you want to puke.

And Melanie did. Her eyes smarted, her head exploded, she retched acid, green bile, toast and peanut butter, with sodden white and yellow tablets. She tried to focus on the vomit but managed to count only two whole yellow and four white tablets before her vision blurred.

She imagined them finding her crumpled body on the bathroom floor, mother, her sister, Dr. Guscott. They'd finally get the picture. Next time he'd answer his phone.

Her knees began to buckle. Her eyes swam. She lurched back to the kitchen and clumsily dialled the library. It's me she said when they'd quickly summoned mother, and then she dropped the receiver.

FOUR

Robert Snow came to in a small bare room, his head on a damp
pillow, his body lying heavily on a hard lumpy mattress on the floor.
The smell in his nostrils was nauseating. It took him back to a
childhood tonsillectomy when he had awakened with his nose and his
brain full of ether, the fumes trapping and holding him.

The small room was green, walls, door, ceiling, all green, the
weak cobalt green of institutions. There were no windows in the
room, only a single door with a bubbled porthole. His head felt raw,
as if all its nerve endings had been laid bare, his whole head a single
giant toothache. Lizard muscles crawled under his skin. The pillow
dampness appeared to be his own, his own sweat and drool, yet his
lips were dry and crusted.

He rolled off the mattress onto the floor, feeling its firmness with
his hands. He was reassured by its tiled reality, and he lay there for a
moment letting the cold seep into his body. He was dressed in a gown
of some sort, a hospital gown, also green, and when he struggled to
his knees the gown fell open at the back. His genitals hung hopelessly
between his legs and when he tried to raise his head his vision began
to close from the sides. His sense of balance faltered and he rolled
back onto the mattress, face upward, mouth open, breathing rapidly.

His eyes itched. He imagined a dry red membrane pasted to them.
From the high ceiling of his cell a single bulb encased in wire mesh
cast an unwelcome sickly light. He wondered then about death and
hell but if this were hell's small room he'd surely have somebody to
talk to while the devil watched from the door. Looking up he saw
eyes behind the bubbled window, distorted but watching him, and he
felt cool paranoia trickle down his spine and constrict his chest.

He struggled to place himself, to name himself. The patterns on
the wall shifted ominously - the last few days, his last week - patches
of memory came to him like falling leaves. He had been lying on his
back as now but in an ambulance, rushing toward his head, in a coffin
speeding down a highway, and before that there had been a jail cell
where a stranger sat screaming in a corner, and before that a room not

much bigger than this room. They had come to a building he could see from his stretcher, and high, wide marble steps leading to an entrance framed by tall columns. He had been carried up like an offering, between railings lined with monks, no, not monks, crows, just sleek watchful crows perched on the railings. It had seemed a mausoleum in the country, somewhere up the Fraser Valley in the direction of Abbotsford and Hope, and he had been carried inside to a high-ceilinged ceremonial room where a priestess in white had leaned over him and then spoken to him.

Exhausted from the effort of remembering, and struggling to keep what he had just remembered, he clutched his penis for comfort. It was something to hold onto, something to protect, and he slipped into a twilight zone, neither asleep nor awake, and let the jumbled colored fragments play on the back of his retina.

"Hello, Mr. Snow. How are you feeling now?"

The door of his prison was open, air was moving, and a woman stood above him, a woman in a white shroud, white coat, open up the front, hands buried in large pockets, the priestess in his dream. He recognized his room now, from his days working the alcohol unit at Maryland State. A bubble room. Seclusion room. A continent-wide feature of mental hospitals. Something like Holiday Inn. Still, familiarity did not bring comfort.

"Are you feeling any better today?"

She towered above him, shoes, low heels, trim ankles, hem of skirt, chin and nose in bottom profile, her legs and hips substantial, her shoulders fading in the distance. She seemed a little uneasy, pulling her hands out of her pockets then replacing them. He remembered his nakedness, the gown bunched across his chest, and quickly assumed the one hand gesture of modesty.

"You're in a hospital, Mr. Snow, Essondale. They brought you here two days ago, from city jail. I'm afraid you've been quite toxic, delirious in fact. We had to let you sleep it off." Her voice was soft, girlish, but precise.

His mind picked up the "mister" and he remembered other times he'd been in hospital as a patient and quickly lost his M.D. He didn't correct her.

She knelt beside him and pulled at the gown to cover his body. "There."

There what? He thought. There you are. All better now. All done?

Still kneeling she asked, "Do you remember much about what happened?"

There was noise, movement, somebody dragging a chair into his room. She flustered, "It's all right, I won't..." but righted herself and sat. He rotated his head to watch her. In the moment she had knelt by him he had detected a fine flower scent doing battle with his own rank odours, and his old childhood companion, shame, perched between them.

"Do you remember much about what happened?"

He looked at the ceiling. "Some."

"Do you know what month it is, Mr. Snow?"

"July. Dog days." He needed a drink.

"I thought dog days was August."

"Maybe so."

"Is it July or August?"

"July."

"And the date?"

"Somewhere in the middle."

"That's close enough. That's fine. I'm Dr. Brennan by the way. I'll be looking after you here."

He relaxed his grip on his genitals and looked more closely at her face. An attractive woman, with tired sympathetic eyes, a fine straight nose, mouth a little thin and prissy. He couldn't tell her age, somewhere between 30 and 40. She could have done more with her hair. She was tall, slim, a model or a matron, or both, in between, becoming a matron.

She asked him about the twitching in his legs. Jumping, he answered, have to move them. He resisted the temptation to use the words akathisia and dystonia and he didn't know why. Maybe he was ashamed to establish himself as a member of the medical fraternity, or sorority. Was he hungry? Thirsty, he answered. Then she got up to stand above him once more, "We'll transfer you to the dormitory in a little while. You won't have to stay in this room much longer, and then we can have a talk."

"Wait."

She turned back. "Yes?"

14

He didn't know why he wanted her to stay. I'm Dr. Robert Snow. Please shoot me. Buy me a drink. Call Jennifer. Instead he heard himself asking, "Why am I still alive?" He was disgusted by the self-pity in his question and he added, "Forget it."

There was a faint smile on her face. "Not your lucky day I guess."

Then she was gone, an older man in white reclaiming the chair, the door closing with a hollow thud.

Pills. He took pills, a bottle of scotch. Painless suicide. And then he remembered the fire escape, crawling naked through the window, sprawling on the iron grate, making ready to jump, shit no, cursing at the buggers in the street, hookers, derelicts, urban Indians, the iron railing coming alive, the brick wall crawling with insects, bums in the street yelling at him, winos ignoring him, the window crashing shut so he couldn't get back in, the world swaying and tilting, and him working up the courage to do it, to jump, yes, to jump once and for all, and splatter the lousy fuckers with his own blood and shit, and watching it, one small part of him watching, staging and choreographing, painting the scene, the high drama of it all, the silliness of it all, and recognizing too late he just wanted Jen to give him another chance, and this was no fucking way to go about it, and if he's lost her he's lost her, his own bloody fault, and then the window flying open, a cop grabbing his ankle, and now him pulling away and trying to jump, really trying to jump, the bastard dragging him back through the window, chest scraping, nose bleeding, puking on one of them, head held under the tap, puking some more, washed off like a child, pants yanked on, balls caught in the zipper, him saying I'm a doctor, I'm a doctor, for Chris' sakes, and the cops saying, sure, doc, sure, and, Jesus, dragging him down the stairs, pushing him in the back of a car, then dragging him out into some emergency room, where he was stretchered, bled, prodded, telling the intern to go fuck himself, intern talking to cops, unhappy cops dragging him back to a car, booking him, relieving him of belt and shoelaces and stuffing him into a foul smelling cell where shadowed quiet descended and his grasp of time and structure collapsed.

FIVE

Snow didn't know how much time had passed. The sparse light remained the same. He'd been able to lie on his side, then crawl, and now he could sit on the mattress if he kept his head low and massaged his legs. Intermittently he heard muffled screaming from somewhere far off but otherwise the institution seemed lifeless. The air was still. He was alternately cold and then hot. His skin flushed and sweated with spasms of shame.

He looked up when the door opened and a man entered, a man in white pants, white jacket, tired looking, about fifty, a man who saw him and didn't see him.

"Put these on, Sarge. I'll be back in a few minutes."

Snow waited until the door was closed again before unrolling the bundle to find a pair of pyjamas. It was then he felt most acutely the absence of his wallet, his watch, anything of his own, anything solid connecting a past life with this incomprehensible present. He struggled out of his gown and put the top on first, his unbathed body defiling the clean, stiff fabric.

The man came back, not in the few minutes promised, but he came back and helped Snow to his feet and led him slowly from the dismal cell. His mind was light and woozy, his vision unclear.

"Where'll it be Sarge, the dormitory or the dayroom?"

"Washroom."

"O.K. Washroom it is. Take it easy now. One step at a time."

They moved slowly down a corridor, turned right and entered a room with 12, 15, maybe 20 beds. They kept to the right along a wall, walked through the room and entered a tiled area with 2 cubicles, sinks, a urinal, shower stall, one small mirror. He made it to the first cubicle and let himself be lowered onto the toilet seat.

"All righ' now." The cubicle had no door, nor had the washroom.

"Give a shout when you're finished." The man turned and walked away.

Snow sat for a long time with his elbows on his thighs, head in his hands. He hadn't said washroom for any particular excretory purpose but rather because he craved something familiar, a place he'd been before, a private activity he understood.

He heard an incongruous clack of heels on the tile floor and looked up to see a face grinning at him around the metal stall. It was the face of a boy, a kid, blue eyes, wispy erratic mustache, long blonde sideburns beneath a brown Stetson.

"Name's Hardy," it said. "Mat Hardy." The face moved away. Snow could hear him on the other side of the stall, running water in a sink.

His voice came over the marble divider. "You bin in the hole, right? Musta bin pretty wild when you come in. Strait jacket the way I hear it."

The water stopped running and the face appeared again, hair slicked back, Stetson in hand. "So you're wondering why I'm here, so I'm gonna tell ya. Full grade certified looney is what I am, a boney fide maniac depressive." The grinning face disappeared again.

"Naw, it's all bullshit," the voice said over more running water, then a loud, prolonged fart. "Speak o' mighty one." The water stopped. "I just get a little paranoid now and again is all. Went off my rock oncet way back but there was good reason for it, man. I mean I just got no place else to go at the moment. No pressing engagements ya might say." The face came back around the edge of the stall. "You wouldn't spot me ten? No? Goddamn quiet bastard. I could pay you back. The old man's got a 20 section spread outside Lethbridge." He returned to the sink. "Can't go back there now. Have to stay in Vancouver this time, find me a stake. Look man, catch you later. It's O.T. and I.T. time and all that shit and I gotta be way the fuck outa here."

Snow sat alone in the hollow silence of the empty washroom. Hardy's presence had come as a surprise to him; he hadn't considered the possibility of other patients. He could hear the odd footstep beyond the washroom now and then, the closing of doors, the scrape of a broom being pushed along the floor, but nothing more to help him believe in the existence of others. The tiles grew cold under his bare feet.

"Finished Sarge?"

A large ring with oversized keys dangled prominently at the attendant's waist.

"Come on, off you come, atta boy. Pull your bottoms up. Pretty sight you are, Sarge. Better lie down in here for a while." His hands lifted Snow's feet onto a bed. Then there was silence again. He wondered about the time, the day. He wasn't aware of Dr. Brennan's presence until she spoke.

"Legs still jumpy?"

He turned his head to see her sitting on a bed several feet away, watching him.

"Christ yes, they're crawling. And my arms."

"That will wear off in time."

"The shakes?"

"The shakes too."

He turned his eyes to the ceiling. "So this is a mental hospital."

"A Mental Health Centre."

"Same difference."

"I suppose."

"Finally."

"Finally?"

"St. Clair Avenue to Water Street. Toronto General to Essondale."

"You've been a patient at Toronto General?"

"Not exactly."

"And your first name. We don't have your first name."

"Robert."

"Well, Mr. Robert Snow, when you're a little better I'll ask you how you've come to this sorry state."

He looked at her but said nothing.

"You said some things in your delirium."

"I imagine."

"Some names. Beth, Elizabeth, Ann and Jennifer. All women's names."

"I don't remember."

"But you know who they are?"

"My daughter, my wife, my..." Lover, ex-girlfriend, happiness that almost was?

"Which is which?"

"In the same order you said them."

"So the last one, Jennifer?"

"Well, I don't really know. A possibility or a fantasy."

18

"Why did you drink so much all at once, and overdose on pills."

"Why does anyone?"

"Well not why then. What led up to it?"

"Stupidity, greed, avarice, guilt, bad luck and a little asshole in a pink suit."

"Fair enough. I'll let you rest today and talk with you tomorrow, Mr. Snow. You're involuntary by the way. Committed for three months at my discretion. So you might want to be a little more explicit in your answers. There'll be a sleeping pill for you if you need it, and some Librium for the jumpiness."

He turned his head back to look at her. She was leaning forward, hands at the side of the bed, ready to leave, her eyes were tired, she looked like she wanted to be somewhere else. Committed. Well, yeah, he didn't exactly drive up in his '92 BMW. Still, the word rang around in his head.

"Wait a minute." He remembered calling her back once before.

"Yes?"

"I...nothing. It doesn't matter."

"I'll talk to you tomorrow then."

Alone again Snow lost track of time. Was it twilight or morning? Had he been lying on this bed a few minutes or several hours? He pulled himself up and, steadying himself on bed railings, made his way to the tall windows along one side of the dormitory. There were no bars on the windows but each individual pane was smaller than a man's shoulders and lay within a heavy metal lattice. He was startled to find himself up a storey or two with a courtyard below, the sun low in the sky on his left, and beyond the courtyard a grassy knoll with pathways leading up to a large brick building fire red and black shadowed in the setting sun, five storeys high, and another on the right, identical to the first, the grass continuing up between and behind them until it reached the edge of a forest. He stared into the distance, into the heavy green. There was a figure far up the hill by the trees, no, two people, tiny, a man and a woman. They were walking on a path beside the forest, he with an arm around her shoulder. Abruptly they moved left and disappeared into the trees. He was exhausted by the time he reached his bed again, and he barely noticed a man in a wheelchair watching him from the corner of the room. Then he dozed and let time slip by.

"You don't look so suicidal."

The voice was coming from where Dr. Brennan had been, and he thought it was his priestess returned, aged, become a witch.

"Maybe you're one of them sex maniacs. A prevert or somethin'."

The woman was worn, bent. Spiteful eyes radiated from deep sockets. Her skin was the color of old picture varnish, her hair thin, unruly, speckled grey, with a fancy comb perched over her left temple. Her mouth was slack against her few blackened teeth, her fingers deeply nicotined, nails crimson and chipped, red smudges on her cheeks. She came over to stand above him. He could see the veins in her eyes.

"Got any smokes? Store bought. Not the shit they dole out in here, pardon my French."

He was able to shake his head no. He wondered for which sin this woman had been sent to haunt him.

"You ain't got nothin' I need then." She moved to the foot of his bed, perched over the edge like a vulture, staring at him. "All alike, ain'tcha, all alike. My second husband per example. Couldn't get it up. Not once in five years...not for me anyhow." She spoke with the raspy, thickened throat of a heavy smoker. "Gettin' it off with his floozies." Her mood changed suddenly. "Tell you a joke. Just a humour joke. This old lady, she says if you can't get it up then just drop it in on your way by. Point of view. I forget the first part. Never mind. My Harry could remember everything. Right to the day he died. I knew what he was up to...you can't fool Bessie, no siree. Maybe just pullin' his own." She made a sucking hacking sound that Snow guessed was laughter, then a long phiizzzz accented by a wave of her hand and a crooked finger that seemed to imply volumes.

He let his gaze drift back to the ceiling. She returned to the side of the bed and held her face just inches above his. "I forgive my Harry. I'm a forgiving person. That's the way I am. That's not a boast, just the way I am." She pointed the crooked index finger at his chest. "You wouldn't cheat on old Bessie would you, sweetie?" She leaned in closer. "How old do you guess I am?"

He knew he would have to speak if he wanted to be rid of the hot strong breath she was blowing in his face. "Fifty," he said.

Her eyes widened. "Fifty...fifty he says." She sat down on the edge of his bed, pulled a small tin from a pocket in her ragged

20

sweater, took out papers, tobacco, began to roll a cigarette, spilling bits on his bed. "With my war paint on I can pass for thirty-nine."

There was hurt in her voice, and pouting, like a child inside a Halloween mask.

"Gotta light?"

He shook his head again.

"Here you are, ma'am."

The cowboy had come back. Maybe he'd been there among the shadows all along. He ignited a wooden match with a snap of his thumbnail and applied it to the woman's cigarette... with a well-practiced flourish Snow thought. He was still wearing his Stetson, and now a purple T-shirt, short sleeves rolled up, the left one over a packet of cigarettes, bare arms well muscled, strong. There was a raw looking M carved or burned like a brand over the exposed upper left arm. He wore a large silver-buckled belt, tight faded jeans and tooled leather western boots.

Bessie seemed to be blowing through her cigarette rather than inhaling. A cloud of smoke and ash gathered around her head.

"Don't pay no attention to old Bessie," said Hardy. "She just don't know up from down."

"Don't you sass me, you young pip squeak. Bessie is nobody's hoor." The cowboy winked at Snow and sauntered away.

"And you," she said, turning back to Snow. "I know your type, the quiet type, but give 'em half a chance and whizzz, faster'n ya can say Jack Robinson. Men, always thinkin' 'bout the same thing. Well, let me tell you a thing or two, sweetie. You won't get Bess to spread her legs, not by a long shot. Time we got treated with a little respect."

"Bessie, what are you doing in the men's dormitory? And smoking too." A nurse was walking toward them from the door.

"Just settin' 'im straight from the start. He better not try anything tonight. Got a knife to bed with me, cut off his whatsits."

"Bessie honey, no one is coming after you tonight. You're perfectly safe." She had Bessie by the arm.

"A lot you know."

"Come on then. I'll take you back to the dayroom."

Bessie got up to follow but suddenly tore away from the nurse and flung herself at Snow. He winced in surprise, pulled his knees up in reflex, expecting pain, embarrassment, but Bessie merely leaned down and planted a sloppy kiss on his forehead. Then she spun around and strode from the room.

He wondered what the fuck he was doing in this looney bin, this funny farm, this insane asylum. He felt fits of anxiety being here, being one of these people, this now his world, and yet...despite his anxiety, his depression, his misery, he found himself smiling, only slightly, but smiling, at Bessie's dignified departure.

He woke in fits and starts, like a man struggling up a hill, climbing and pausing, hauling himself over the final edge, heart pounding wildly. His eyes opened before he left his dream. He was in the dark, haunted by remnants of memory, a small boy in danger with no strength in his arms or legs, searching for light to orient himself. There was a little from the windows, grey, gauze-filtered, and from the door to the corridor, yellow, quiet.

Now wide-awake, acutely awake, he recognized the post- drunk clarity of his mind. He scanned the room - high ceiling, its definition lost in shifting, murky ghost-like images, deep shadows in the corners of the room, half visible human forms huddled in attitudes of remorse.

A shadow, a man sat up in bed picking at his blankets with uncertain fingers, fingers that seemed to represent some break in the chain of command, moving sightlessly, and unsuccessfully, searching, picking.

Hardy lay two beds over from Snow, apparently comatose or drugged, his breathing open-mouthed and stertorous, louder than the other bodies who emitted only snuffles, groans, the occasional cough, bedsprings squeaking in reply.

Snow noticed he was under a blanket - a nurse must have tucked him in - and he felt its weight as a prison. He pulled on it, flung it aside, sat up with a start and then carefully lay back again to quell the sudden sensation of weightlessness, fearing he might roll or lift off his small hard bed. He pressed himself into the mattress, arms and legs spread like a pinned specimen. Hardy rolled in his sleep and spoke in the intense inward manner common to dreamers, "...take it with you, don't want it no more." And then after a pause, "Stop it, for Chris' sake, stop it."

Snow turned onto his stomach attempting to curl into the mattress as one might curl around a body, but it had no give to it and refused to become Jennifer. Face down, nose into the pillow, he grew aware of the damp, cold, unyielding quality of his bed and the faint odour of urine that permeated the room, and the thick acrid sweetness of the sweat of the mentally ill.

The light flickered in the hallway as somebody passed outside the open door and he could just make out a conversation between two women, one voice placating, irritated, the other young, petulant.

"Why aren't you in bed, Melanie?"

"I couldn't sleep. I was having this awful dream. Could I have another pill...please?"

"Dr. Dromore didn't order anything else, Melanie, but you can come to the dayroom and I'll get you a glass of milk."

"Ugh, I hate milk. It reminds me too much of mother's milk."

"Melanie..."

"It's true. I can remember, especially when Dr. Guscott hypnotizes me. He says I've got a sexual identity problem, like David Bowie. Are you sure I can't have another pill? I really have to get some sleep. I feel like my brain is falling out of my head or something."

"No more pills, Melanie. You can come down to the desk to talk awhile if you'd like but that's it."

"I think the back half of my brain is taking over the front half. That's the part that has the anger you know, the back half, it's just swallowing the front half. I can hear it moving. Do you think I'm smart?"

"Of course, of course I do, Melanie."

"I wish you'd stop calling me Melanie."

"It's your name."

"I don't like it. I've never liked it. How about Camille...or Francine, something a little older, more mature, a little wicked."

"It's time you went back to bed, Melanie."

"I can't sleep in this horrid place. Dr. Guscott used to always put me in the General when I overdosed before. Maybe he's given up on me."

"Shh. I don't think so, Melanie. He wouldn't do that."

"Oh yes he would. He thinks he's so darn clever. I hate him you know, I really do."

"Now keep your voice down, Melanie. We don't want to wake anybody."

"I don't care. They're all crazy anyway. Just one little pill, Frieda, come on, just one, then I'll go right to bed."

Pills, thought Snow as the voices faded, magic pills, and then he thought of his own alcohol, his own need, and his mind filled with memories, doubts and regrets, anger at himself for past decisions and past lassitude, stupidity, and he craved sleep to anaesthetize himself. A pressure welled behind his eyes and he broke out in a cold sweat, listening to his skipping heart, feeling the burning fever in his ears. He tried to think of pleasant things, beautiful women, a warm beach, but these, ephemeral as always, failed to stem the tide of remorse, the critical examination of his failings, still going on after all these years. From this there was no asylum in the asylum.

SIX

"Been here three times. This one makes three. And two times before that in Ponoka and once in Edmonton. Ponoka's a hole and Edmonton's no better. If you gotta spend time in a looney bin this place ain't bad."

Snow felt foolish sloppily dressed in pyjamas and disposable slippers, the bottoms pulled high and left to prevent his whatsits from flopping out, his remnants of dignity. He tried to make himself small in the large green vinyl armchair spotted with cigarette burns, in the corner of the dayroom, but the cowboy had drawn up a chair directly in front, straddled it, and proceeded to talk as if to an old friend.

"You get a little freedom here, privileges they call it, walk the grounds and things, smoke a little dope in the bushes. Course you ain't got no privileges yet, got your pink ass in jammies, but Brennan's pretty easy, get your clothes back soon enough." He picked at his front uppers with the nail of his thumb. "Calgary a week ten days ago, cattle auction, the old man's back started acting up so he sent me up to Calgary to look over the breeding stock. The place was crawling with dudes man, smart asses, oil money, ruining the goddamn place, oil money, cops everywhere, gambling, and me with two thou' in my pocket."

The cowboy stretched his legs, tilted the brown Stetson to the back of his head, glanced around the room, then returned to his story. A few patients sat on the periphery of the large day room staring into its empty middle. The high windows and dated quality reminded Snow of a train station.

"...I had to get out of there man, too close, y'know, creeping in on ya, watching, always watching, kep' my hands in my pockets all the time. Blew the old man's money on the down payment for a hot little Transam and took off for Vancouver. Whoosh, V 8, twin cam, headers, Jesus. Figured on gettin' a job on the coast or maybe just live on the beach for a while, you know, let things sorta cool down. Picked up a chick in Banff, sweet little thing with big bazooms, and flogged that sucker non-stop through the Rockies. Whew-eee, what a trip,

straight through Roger's pass, a case of beer in the back seat, this little
tight blowing me all the way, coming round them corners, me sucking
on the beer, pissin' into the empties, chuck 'em out the window. Just
flyin' man."

A table tennis game was being started in the solarium at the far end
of the day room. The old woman, Bessie, sat hunched and quiet in a
chair on the opposite wall. Ten feet from her was a man in a
wheelchair reading a book, smoking, looking up now and then to stare
in Snow's direction. Snow held his hands between his legs to steady
them, then returned his eyes to Hardy. The boy seemed to want
nothing more than an audience.

"Cops got onto me by then, must've picked up my trail in Banff.
Jesus, was I getting paranoid. Breathin' down my neck, I could feel
'em. So I gotta keep goin', just drove. Ten hours straight drivin' man."
He grasped an imaginary steering wheel, pulled it back and forth. "I
was so pissed and beat and high when I reached Vancouver I didn't
know up from down. First thing was get rid of the chick. Did she put
up a fight, like she couldn't tear herself away from me or som'in. Had
to give her the rest of my money to get rid of her, dumped'er at the
corner of Granville and Georgia, somewheres.

"So there I am see, no money left, no place to go, tried to get into a
flop house on Granville, down by the bridge, but a lotta queers round
there and the paranoid was gettin' to me. Cops again. I figured they
radioed ahead, the make of the car and stuff. Bastards. One of the
queers was undercover, sure as hell. So then I figured I might as well
have it out with them right then and there. I mean if they're following
me all over the fucking place I might as well face 'em down. Y'see it?
I'd take the whole lot of 'em at once. Drive straight to the cop shop,
y'know, down by Hastings and Main, maybe pick up a piece on the
way." Hardy pulled his Stetson forward, jumped his chair a little
closer to Snow and assumed a conspiratorial whisper. "So I drives
down Main Street and pull up right in front of the station, double
park, and then I realize I forgot to get the gun. Brennan says I didn't
wanna get a gun and maybe that's true. Anyway, before I could get
out, this cop comes over to the car, he's a big bugger, and asks me to
pull ahead, y'know, waves me ahead. The car window's open on my
side, so I figure I'll stick 'm with my Bowie-knife when he comes
close enough, ain't really a Bowie-knife, it's straight, but both edges
are sharp as piss, carry it in my right boot, see. So I bend down to get

26

it out and what the fuck you think happens? I puke all over myself, is
what happens. Puke all over myself. Bang my head on the steering
wheel and puke all over myself. Jesus H. Christ. I ain't thinkin' now.
So I jump out the car cursin', pull my boots off to keep the puke from
runnin' in, hoppin' around, and out falls the knife. Game over. I mean
I assume the position before he even asks."

Snow found himself listening, almost absorbed, forgetting for a
moment his sleepless night, the wire band around his head.

Dr. Brennan walked into the day room, glanced in their direction
and passed on, stopping to talk with the man in the wheelchair, then a
young boy, then Bessie, each one following her as she moved on to
the next, like rats and the Pied Piper. Drowning rats. He felt left out,
ignored, considered this, and filed it in the scrap heap of misleading
emotions, scorning any real hope in the few seconds she bestowed on
each of them.

"The bugger slams my head against the car, still got the bruise,
right here, see. Then he sticks the cuffs on and hustles me into the
station. They put me in a holding cell and there I sit, stinking of puke.
I hate cells man. The walls start comin' in on me and I know I gotta
do somethin' or I'll really go off the deep end. So I take off my
clothes and start to rip 'em into little pieces. That's what I do. I mean I
gotta do som'in' eh? I'm sitting there tearin' 'em up, stark naked. Some
cop comes by sees me doing this so he calls the others over to take a
look. There I am bare assed with all these cops staring at me so I spit
at 'em through the bars. Well that cuts it. They jump me pretty quick
and put me in a strait jacket. The jail's got an old wino quack working
there and he fills me full of shit with a horse needle and they send me
out here. Wham. Back in the looney bin. Who needs it? This place is
full of whackos. They're all two bricks short of a load, the elevator
don't reach the top floor, know what I mean? So Brennan wants to put
me on this lithium business, says it'll even out the bumps in my ego.
Skinny bitch could do with a few bumps herself." Momentarily run
down, he glanced around the dayroom, and Snow watched a
surprising change of mood. The cowboy's bravado slipped from his
face like wax melting in the sun and left - what? Loneliness and fear?
Sadness? Then it changed again, the energy back, the smile broad,
eyes alive. "There's Melanie, they musta let her outa the bubble room.
Hey Mel, over here." But the slight blonde girl drifted by, as if

nursing some very personal tragedy, hearing Hardy, Snow was sure, but making him get up and follow her.

"Shit." Hardy untangled himself from the chair, caught up with the girl and led her back to the doorway, arm around her shoulder. Snow could hear their conversation as they went past.

"Jeanie's gone missing."

"Prob'ly run off to Vancouver," said Hardy.

"She didn't take her jacket."

"Yeah, well, she'll be back."

The table tennis game had fizzled out. A high morning sun slanted through the windows, casting bar shadows, exposing dust in the air and stains and cigarette burns on the linoleum floor. He squeezed the bridge of his nose between thumb and middle finger, trying to clear his eyes, improve their focus. A large section of the end wall was glass, like a picture window, or a ticket counter, and behind the glass there was movement, a face looking out on the dayroom.

A loud speaker crackled into life. "Robert Snow to the nursing station." The message was repeated.

Snow looked up, startled. He didn't know what to make of it. A woman approached, a nurse, perhaps an aide, "Dr. Brennan would like to see you now, Robert, in her office, just down the corridor. Come along now"

She was taking him by the arm as if he were an errant child, or a very old man. He clung to his pyjama bottoms with his free hand, losing his right slipper, regaining it, shuffling along. He felt he had aged ten years or more and become an object of scorn and pity.

"Well, Mr. Snow, you do look better." She was shaking his hand as if they were meeting for the first time. She had a small slim hand, and she was almost as tall as he, taller unless he managed to straighten his spine, look her in the eye. "Have a seat." She settled into a chair behind the desk.

It was a small room with a single wire-meshed window behind her head, creating a halo effect. He felt vulnerable.

"I feel foolish sitting here in pyjamas."

"I understand, we'll get you back in street clothes very soon." She waited, watching him with kind, concerned eyes, perhaps a little wary. He felt his mouth go dry, his head empty of its knowledge, his energy seeping away.

"Perhaps we can start by you telling me about the last week or so."
She fiddled with a pen, not as if she were about to write, more a
nervous mannerism.

The past week, drinking, day into night, sickness, yearning, then
hopelessness, not a week, just a coda, the big out become a big folly.
He said, "I don't remember very much."

"You don't usually drink that heavily?"

"I've been known to."

"Have you been hospitalised for it before, or in a detox centre?"

"A treatment centre."

"Where?"

"Toronto and Atlanta."

"Atlanta? Isn't that..."

"I'm a physician as well as an alcoholic."

She put down her pen and looked at him. He said, "I'm not
delusional."

"Okay. I'll go with it. How does a, what, a Toronto physician end
up a John Doe on Water Street in Vancouver?"

"They don't have a very high success rate."

"Obviously."

"It's a boring story."

"I have a few minutes."

"I lost my licence in Toronto. The Addiction Foundation and the
Ontario College sent me to the Atlanta Treatment Centre for six
months. When I was sober for six months I looked around for a
supervised institutional job, something the College would approve,
and got accepted as director of the alcohol treatment program at
Maryland State. The alcohol business is one field where we've
achieved excellent consumer participation in management as you
probably know." He continued when she didn't smile. "Anyway, some
very strange things happened during my year there and I fell off the
wagon once, maybe twice, just a day or two each time. In the end the
medical director sent a shitty report to the College and they voted to
continue my suspension. I did what a drunk does when he's
disappointed. I got drunk. The woman I was living with, who'd taken
me in I guess, she kicked me out. Our deal was zero tolerance. So I
was out on the street. So I joined all the drunken and substance
abusing lemmings and headed west to throw myself in the sea."

"And you really wanted to kill yourself?"

"I don't know. Yes. Maybe. I tried to reach Jennifer but she wouldn't talk with me."

"The woman you lived with."

"Yes. She gave up. I gave up."

"You needed her to rescue you?"

"A steadfast, caring, forgiving mother?"

"Well?"

"No. Christ. I don't know. The nipple, the bottle, I'm too old for this kind of shit."

"Well, you did lose more than a woman. Your profession, your dignity, your livelihood, your identity."

"That's true."

"And you may have a depression."

"It runs in the family.'

"So this may not be entirely an infantile need run amok."

"You're very kind."

"You're still involuntary."

He waited for her to continue but the phone on her desk interrupted. He watched her face as she answered. "No, it's all right...How long has it been?..Well...I don't know...I didn't think she was suicidal...Have we done any kind of search of the grounds?...Well, she's missing from here, how long before the police consider her missing, I mean their kind of missing?...All right, I guess that's all we can do."

She hung up and turned back to Snow. "I'm sorry. What was I saying? Oh yes. Your status. You haven't asked to be made voluntary."

"Would you do that?"

"I don't know yet."

"Well, I'm not actually in any hurry to be free."

She moved her chair around to the corner of the desk, leaned a little closer, head tilted to her right, eyebrows raised. Her hands were folded demurely in her lap, a white lab coat hid her figure, but there was a fragile elegance to her. She asked him about his bowels, his sleep, his weight, his energy level, (all down he said, rock bottom), his interest in things, people, did he feel any hope?

He could see no threat in this woman and yet against his better judgement, or perhaps no longer trusting his judgement, he guarded himself. He quelled the tears that rose to his eyes. He willed restraint

30

in the shaking hand that wanted to reach out. He rubbed his eyebrows, managed a smile with his lips alone, though he knew it would appear sardonic. He had to talk about something or he'd soon be crying in her arms. But again the telephone rescued him.

"Yes...I am busy...I'm seeing someone...no, I understand...go ahead, it's all right...damn...I suppose I've got to come and see him, you can't hold him for 30 minutes or so, I mean he's in his wheelchair isn't he. He can't really leave without help...yes, I know, he can be very difficult...okay, tell him I'll be there in just a few minutes, hide his crutches or something, no, better not do that, I'll be there in just a minute."

She turned back to Snow and he watched her compose her face, and once more, if only for a minute, offer him her full attention. "I'm sorry, Dr. Snow, I have to attend to something on the ward. I think this will take us some time at any rate. We can continue tomorrow." She made no move to stand and seemed to be considering something.

Snow listened to his own shallow breathing, still inhaling, exhaling, his own breath, his own mind, saved by the telephone from the soft seduction of Essondale's mistress.

"I think you do have a depression, Dr. Snow. Things look very bleak to you now but I know you can be feeling much better in a few weeks. It will all look different to you then. I'm prescribing antidepressant medication to give you some energy and improve your mood." She caught herself and smiled. "Do you have a preference?"

Snow shook his head and watched impassively as she unfolded what he was sure were ice-cold hands, hid them in the pockets of her white laboratory coat and ushered him from her office.

SEVEN

He awoke in the early morning, before any light. A dream still lingered in his drug-clouded consciousness. The dream was clear and reclaimed him.

He had felt guilty and looked guilty and he hated her for making him so, Ann, his wife. She did this with a simple look, a posture, a hurt expression, accusing eyes, a cadence in her voice. His mind played tricks on him, tried to alter the facts. Sometimes it succeeded. More often the truth hung between them like a blood-red carcass.

The dialogue came back to him - the dialogue in which he focused attention on distracting elements, altering guilt, wringing from it righteousness and cynicism, offering forgiveness for insults not yet tendered.

"You're late."

"Ummmph."

"I put Elizabeth to bed."

"Is she asleep yet?"

"Of course. Do you know how late it is?"

He doesn't look at her. His face is burning with shame and regret.

"You've been drinking again."

He must find a way to the bathroom to wash in cold water - to wash the smell of sex from his nostrils. "I'll go up and say goodnight."

"I called your office." Her eyes are small again, reduced to tiny accusing slits, surrounded by unsightly puffiness. She is unattractive, deliberately unattractive he thinks, and hates his lack of generosity.

"I had to go over to the hospital." He knows they'll play this out without ever saying what really lies between them. He's terrified of her rage, or of the horror it may induce in him. She's afraid of something too. Of what he hasn't known for some time. He once thought it was loss, loneliness, hearing the truth. Now he thinks they fear the same thing. She doesn't want to view the fierce hatred in the casket of her soul. So opposite her vision of herself. These bloody women expect to be prized and worshipped. They seek specialness. They deny lust and ambition and hate. They fuck us over with moral superiority.

"I'll go up and see Beth." He punctuates the conversation by turning away.

That night they lie back-to-back, making a suburban beast with two fronts, carefully but casually not touching. The room is oppressive. There is clothing on a chair, clothing hanging out of opened drawers, clothing on the floor, half completed curtains draped on the window - her job - part of the woodwork green, part white - his job. Everything started, nothing completed. All postponed because of sudden dissipation of moral rectitude. Or conviction. Conviction is needed to paint woodwork and sew curtains.

He lies beside her thinking. Even then he knows his mind is not letting him see the whole story. Like a multiple image screen with several key sectors blacked out. He thinks about his behavior and despairs of ever finding a direct connection between thinking and feeling.

She isn't to be reached tonight and he can't dwell on where he's just been. That too must be shut out. Tomorrow it will all seem less important against the comforting backdrop of habit. But he knows comfort is illusion. Time will only enshrine the chasm that lies between them. Now it might be bridged if he dares. Tonight his guilt could be shed in a painful but healing catharsis. Tomorrow it becomes a permanent hair shirt, buttoned with the small ceramic glances of her anxiety, of her hurt and of her loathing.

She once asked, "What's the matter? Tell me what the matter is."

And got no answer.

And he shed tears in the dark, knowing all the while the tears were gratifying. He wore them the way a poet wears his solitude and his poverty. All so goddamned seriously.

"Would you check on Elizabeth please? Her breathing doesn't sound very good." She's been lying awake, facing the other way, listening to the house.

"She's fine...just has a cold."

"It sounds very deep to me, and she complained of headaches today."

"She's all right. I listened to her before coming to bed. Her breathing's fine. Just croup."

"Are you sure it hasn't gotten into her chest?"

"Yes, I'm sure."

He has rolled onto his back and opened his eyes to watch the
shifting street lamp patterns on the ceiling. Now he hears the child's
breathing reaching into his own anxieties. He gets up and walks
around the bed and down the hall to Elizabeth's room. He picks up her
small body and carries her to the bathroom. She wakes groggily and
clings to his neck when he reaches over to turn on the shower. He sits
on the lid of the toilet seat with the child in his arms as the room fills
with steam. The dry rasping intake of her breathing changes
gradually, first to something softer and then, after a coughing spell, to
a clear and clean passage of air...He carries her back, asleep already in
his arms, and leaves her on her bed. It is a moment when everything
in the world is clear. Gratifying and miraculous. And he knows he
will run from it.

Early that morning they made love, as they often did, trying to
regain with their bodies that which their minds had lost. But she was
aware of his effort to recapture some feeling, some connection, with
every clumsy stroke, and afterward, looking into her eyes, he saw her
searching his face for something no longer there.

EIGHT

"This is Karpov," said Hardy. "He's Bulgarian."

It was late afternoon the day after Snow's session with Brennan. Two days out of seclusion he was still in pyjamas, or maybe three days. Time behaved differently in here, crawling sluggishly between infrequent reference points. Hardy had assumed the job of guiding Snow through the labyrinth of institutional life. "Karpov wants to see you," he had said, and had led Snow to a corner of the day room where a man in a wheelchair was waiting.

Karpov was a slight man. His lower face was hidden behind a large unruly black beard, a Rasputin beard Snow would come to think. His thin black hair was slicked back from his high balding forehead, a head that looked too big for his body. His black eyes displayed a hint of madness. He didn't seem to blink.

Snow realized this was the man who had been watching him from the corner of the dormitory, a cripple in his wheelchair, but not just any wheelchair he noticed now, for from its tarnished chrome, securely fixed with string and ribbon, hung transparent plastic bags containing all the things a man might need to get him through the day: a set of keys, a thermos bottle, a small ashtray, cigarette papers, a pouch of tobacco, matches, a small wrench, a bottle opener, tissues. Two hardcover books were stuffed between his left leg and the arm of the chair, a newspaper in a slot at his back.

The Bulgarian accentuated his gaze with luxurious drags on a crudely made cigarette, pinching it between the thumb and forefinger of his right hand, palm cupped under his chin, as if the object were both perfect and distasteful, sometimes switching to his ring and middle finger, using the cigarette as part of his language, his dramatic gestures.

"I speak Bulgarian, Russian, French, English, German, and a little Greek. And Turkish." He told Snow. "The Turks have always been our enemies, one had to know Turkish." Blue smoke swirled above his head. The cigarette flared and danced. "They left us coffee and corpses. When we finally drove them out."

Snow sat heavily in the chair Hardy indicated for him, somewhat surprised by his curiosity, a state of mind he considered as outdated as virginity.

"Dostoyevsky," announced Karpov, pronouncing the name with authentic guttural o's and a thickened v. "Dostoyevsky searched for the perfectly good man, but found him only in Christ, as he knew he must. Of course to understand Dostoyevsky you must read Notes From The Underground." He looked off in the distance and quoted, "We are all divorced from life, we are all cripples, every one of us." He stared at Snow as if waiting for some kind of confirmation.

"I only know Crime and Punishment." He felt uncultured, uneducated, unread, a sham, the physician as technician, no longer a man of letters.

"Of course you would, of course." His eyes seemed to focus just behind Snow's head. "I have read Crime and Punishment five times and still I experience the sheer terror of it, the tension that rips at the very soul of poor Raskolnikov. Why did he need to kill and why did he need to confess, eh? Guilt. Before he killed. He had it before he killed. To kill was the necessary and heroic act, to complete what he already know of himself."

Karpov looked down and lowered his voice as if he were about to share a disagreeable secret. "The ending is very bad, very bad. He should have suicide. It is the only way to end such a journey. Sartre would have known that. My friend Jean-Paul would have had Raskolnikov, - how is it said? - sodomize the corpse of the old lady and then slit his own throat." He looked heavenward at this point and raised his baritone voice. "But those Russians are Romantics, every last one of them. They plunder, they steal, they lie, they kill and yet still they search for truth. They don't believe they could survive without a czar or a committee of czars and yet they are cynical, for cynicism is the first defence of the truly romantic. But they should look at themselves to discover there is no truth, no honesty, no happy endings. Of course I am romantic too, the last Bulgarian romantic."

"Karpov writes poetry," said Hardy.

"It is nothing. Small things. I will show you some later." He inhaled smoke, blew it skyward. "Now Tolstoy was an aristocrat and Dostoyevsky a peasant, but both were romantics, 19th century romantics, and who could be a romantic today, except Karpov, poet, philosopher, lover of mankind. And you see I know as they that

change can only come through the tension of opposites, goodness
from suffering, greatness from struggle, deprivation. Do you know
Siddarthra? No? It is an eastern thought as well. Life must grow from
two opposing forces, simple life, only life, that is all, and love, not
Nietche's superman, merely a whole man, a man who can love and
who will let others love him."

He paused to take a long drag on his cigarette, exhaled slowly
and stared at Snow.

"My name is Robert," said Snow, seeking a way to blunt the
man's gaze.

"It is not necessary," said Karpov, "to know your name. I know
from your eyes that you are sympatico, someone who understands
these things. Now Tolstoy was never happy with his creations and yet
Ivan Ilych is a great piece of art, crafted perfectly."

Snow nodded.

"More truly a novelette," said Karpov, "about a misspent life
summed up in the final weeks of dying. It is not the best time to learn
these things." The loose end of his cigarette flared dangerously. He
stubbed it in his ashtray and then, without pausing, pulled makings
from the pouches attached to his chair and began to roll another.
"Myself, I have learned these things many years ago. I am devoting
my life to love, to agape, for it is through the gift of love that one
achieves immortality and flies with the angels. We must rise above
material things." His tongue snaked out of his beard to wet the glue on
the small white roll. "I have given everything away."

He patted and smoothed the new cigarette while he spoke. "Do
you know I once taught Russian literature at the university, and one
day I asked them, the course review committee, in your Canada you
have committees for everything, I asked them if I could teach a course
from my heart, something that would transcend academic pettiness...
I would call it Immortality Now. At first they agreed to my proposal. I
would tell my students of the journey all great men have taken. I
would engage them in Socratic dialogue and open their minds to the
approximation of truth. Do not misunderstand. I do not profess to
know the truth. I only know that man must search for truth at the
juncture of his reason and his passion. Descartes did not understand
this. It is the tension between reason and passion that germinates life.
The Godhead, it is a...a confluence, not a single point." He struck a
match on the underside of his wheelchair, cupped it to the cigarette in

his mouth and puffed gingerly while the loose bits fell in his lap. "Of course they changed their collective minds. They wanted to preview my source material, sit in on my classes, assign a senior department member to guide me. They are fools without courage. I do not need them. Not Victor Karpov. I need no one. I can curse in seven languages my friend and do not underestimate that gift." Like miniature fireworks angry smoke and bits of red ash puffed from the end of his cigarette. "We must drink together some night, for then we can talk. Today I am not so strong."

But Karpov talked on for an hour in the corner of the dayroom and Snow tuned in and out, his mind falling behind several sentences, nodding now and then with a politeness not yet eroded, his eyes drifting to Hardy still squatting against the wall, and then to the few other patients in the dayroom. They were sitting in silence, one making repeated trips to the window of the nursing station to plead and be rejected. The afternoon amber light slanted through the large south windows, to Ivan Ilych lying on his couch, lying to himself, the horrid truth of moral failure seeping into his flesh like thick grey mould.

On two occasions a nurse or an aide came over and stood for a few minutes beside the group, listening, and then returned to the station. He could imagine her writing on a chart or in a log: 1600 hours; Snow, Karpov and Hardy interacting verbally.

He returned his attention to Karpov, who seemed capable of continuing his...his what? It wasn't conversation. Lecture, monologue, perhaps soliloquy...He wondered what Hardy was listening to? The boy, garrulous and restless a few days ago, was now silent and reverent.

On the chance there was a message in Karpov's ramblings he struggled to clear the thickening in his mind, but his eyes recoiled from the poet's intensity, and his body began to ache for solitude. He was not distressed to hear the call to dinner.

"Would you please wheel me to the lavatory first," Karpov said to Hardy who had quickly taken his position behind the Bulgarian's chair, and then to Snow, "We will talk later you and I. Here, you may look at these." He handed Snow a small sheath of papers.

Snow ate with the other patients not yet trusted off the ward, or too demented to find their way back. Several tables were pulled out from the wall, chairs placed around them, and trays put on the tables by attendants. Snow sat himself across from a confused old man who dribbled milk down his dry and hoary chin, and a woman who did everything in threes. Her attention flickered between the food in front of her and an empty spot above the surface of the table. She touched each utensil three times, and moved the cabbage, and bits of ham, and mashed potatoes to her mouth three times again before finally letting the fork cross her lips.

"Take the fork, Jack. Say hello. Say thank you. Eat the cabbage. Say fuck you, Jack. Say I'm sorry." A young man at the far end seemed to be talking directly to his own mind, like a computer dumping its program. At the other end sat a man in his middle years, worry moving about his face like the tracery of a Jackson Pollock brush. His tremulous right hand touched his face, then his chest, back to his mouth, then his hair.

Snow ate mechanically, without taste, grateful only for the glass of milk to soothe his increasingly dry mouth. He thought of Karpov. The Bulgarian had called himself a semi-quad, yet could use his hands, which meant paraplegia rather than quadriplegia. Perhaps he wished to emphasize the dead half of his body. Semi-quad seemed to imply an incomplete quadriplegia. And why is he here? His ramblings - wisdom or insanity? Or both? And Jesus. What the fuck am I doing here? Sitting all afternoon listening to the ravings of a mad Bulgarian. Am I now one of these, these poor dements dribbling, counting and dumping? But he realized he had neither will nor energy to plan the future or reconstruct the past and that left only the godforsaken present, with its only one lingering anticipation, its one hope - Jennifer. Yet he knew he must rescue himself this time, sort out his own shit first, and then perhaps go to her, and then maybe he'd be worthy of her. And would she still be there? Mashed potato slipped off the fork held in his unsteady hand and slithered into his lap. Nobody at the table noticed. He jiggled it onto the floor.

After eating he looked at Karpov's scribblings, his small things. He began to read the first and then put them away.

Medusa, goddess of the rock
Lying in wait, as all the others
I have loved. You eat, you eat my soul,
My heart. You gather me in and spit me out.

The man of love, of agape had some misogynist anger in his heart.

Several hours later, after the loud speaker announced pill parade, and after they had all lined up and received their pills, after some desultory television, and after the 10 p.m. bedtime was announced, Snow saw Karpov sitting alone in his wheelchair at the far end of the corridor. He was just inside the door to the outside world, his head slumped on his chest, a long-ashed cigarette forgotten between his fingers. Karpov looked up, saw Snow watching him, and smiled. It was a forced, strained smile, almost a grimace. Snow looked away.

And at that moment Snow saw the truth of the semi-quad in all his desolate loneliness, locked in a fractured body, reduced by the corridor shadows, sagging like a puppet without a master, yearning for metaphysical wings and someone who might see him as he wished to be.

NINE

Melanie felt what? Strange, excited, overpowered, passive? Something. Professor Dromore was so strong, so clever. She was seeing him three, sometimes four times a week. Between sessions she got it straight in her mind: he was a shrink and a middle-aged, slightly overweight man. He was also pompous. But in the sessions in his office, when he stared at her, and nodded, and said uh huh, and what a sad life you've had, and called her Melanie, Melanie, and explained to her, her mind went to mush. He was trying to help her, he wanted to help her. He could protect her, and boy did she need it. In his presence she could hardly put a sentence together. And between their sessions her life was still going downhill.

So when he told her her basic problem was a fear of true genital intimacy she had to agree. Yeah. All that other stuff was kid stuff, oral, groping. She had sexual tension to deal with, and that's why she cut her arms, to make a vaginal wound, and when she slept around she was avoiding intimacy, and she was avoiding intimacy because she feared domination. So when he told her that's what she had to learn to deal with, the shadow she had to confront, it made good sense.

Yes, it was all so simple. Dr. Dromore would order her to do things and she would argue but obey. Small things. Fetch that book. Sit over there. Sit up straight. And he was right. It felt good to be told what to do. Between sessions as well, what to wear, what to do, what to tell people about her therapy. When she asked a question he told her she had no right to ask questions. He was in charge. Professor Dromore. He told her what to wear when she came to the sessions. Little girl outfits. She didn't have much to choose from, so mostly she wore her shorts, a pink top and her hair tied up.

Then one day he asked, no, told her to sit on his lap. She hesitated. He explained the beauty of their relationship, all safe transference and counter transference. They could have all the feelings. They could play act some of them and it was all safe. There was no danger here. He was her doctor. She was his patient. No harm could come to her in their relationship so she could learn to have those feelings she avoided, she denied, she repressed, those true genital sexual feelings, have them and learn they were safe and good to have.

She sat on his lap and felt his small erection pressing into her buttock. It's all right, he said. It's all right.

He had her kneel before him and pick up a book in one session, and then just kneel there the next session, eye level with his fly, while he stroked her hair and soothed her. And the next session when she knelt before him his fly was undone and his cock emerged like a small mushroom. Touch it he commanded her. Touch it with your hand. Now touch it with your tongue. Now touch it with your lips. She wasn't new to this and did it well though she wasn't sure what her feelings should be. Before he came he called her a rotten filthy whore and grabbed her head and flung her from him. She grovelled on the floor before him and then rested, spent, on the carpet. He told her he would see her the same time tomorrow but this time she was to enter his office and, without a command from him, take off her top and her bra and stand before him. Between their sessions she opened new wounds on her arms and hid them beneath the sleeves of her shirt. He was right, she was dirt. He was right, she was wrong. Yet in her head she fought him and was drawn to fight him. And then give in to him, this father, this lord and master.

TEN

Snow sat alone on the toilet of an open, doorless cubicle, his bare feet on the cold tile floor, his pyjama bottoms around his cold ankles. He felt very little, not even the comfort of evacuating, plugged up by the pills or his own wilful constipation. Rain gusted against the high barred window. The ward was dark and quiet and the tiled floor was wet under his feet.

He rubbed his tired sex, struggling to conjure a satisfying memory, a living sensation. A bird's eye image came of Jennifer in the tub, her legs spread in the soapy water, her head back, her mouth slack, the fingers of her right hand between her legs, his hand on hers. The image excited his brain but his sex was numb. He rubbed some more as a child rubs himself, achieving scant solace. His right hand quickly tired from the effort. His cock was swollen slightly, just enough to leave it resting on the damp porcelain rim of the toilet bowl.

A shadow appeared and Snow, once ashamed of jerking off, once fearful of someone seeing his shame, finds he cares no longer. He does nothing to hide himself.

The shadow becomes Hardy, who stands before Snow, picking sleep from his eyes. As Snow watches, wondering what should happen next, Hardy drops to his knees and without a word, takes Snow's cock in his mouth. Snow sees the blonde hair, scarred arms, the large roughened hands, and pushes himself back away from Hardy's face but he is blocked by the tank of the toilet, the plumbing against his back. He is afraid of Hardy, his steer-roped hands, his sun bleached hair, his muscled shoulders. He grasps the railing on the cubicle wall to keep himself from touching the boy and closes his eyes. Against himself he swells and hardens in Hardy's mouth, his stomach revolts in agony, confusion, and sex. He opens his eyes and comes, face contorted, expulsing in relief and horror.

Hardy sits back on the tiled floor, looking up at Snow, grinning with his glistening mouth, smiling madly, his lips wet and swollen. "Next best thing to Jeanie," he says. "Jesus, it's cold in here. Come on back to the dorm."

Snow stares at him and shakes his head no. "Leave me," he says. "Go away." He bows his head and covers himself with his hands.

"Yeah. Okay. Suit yourself."

Snow listens to Hardy gargle and spit into the sink on the other side of the cubicle wall and then pad back to the dorm. Sitting there, knees locked together, bent double, arms across his thighs, he thinks of his failings, not cocksucking in the can, not fucking on the toilet seat, but his inability to reciprocate, his failure to offer the cowboy anything, his understanding that he couldn't even act out of kindness, as he failed to offer Jennifer the small certainty she needed. Jennifer now raising two children alone.

When he sleeps alone this night he sleeps the sleep of the paranoid and the damned. He dreams of his flesh falling away from his skeleton, his eyes blinded and seeping. He is lying alone on a vast grey plain, crawling toward an ever-receding horizon. Somewhere in the distance is not Jennifer but this girl he has never seen before, Jeanie, crawling away from him as she bleeds to death.

ELEVEN

Marjorie was sitting in the nursing station doing her charts, pulling them one at a time from the rack, updating orders, writing notes in the progress section. The room was hot. A small fan in the corner helped very little. Frieda was there, smoking, her small metal ashtray inside a drawer for quick disposal should a supervisor happen by, and Paul, a slight, sweet man with an accent. Paul was a natural. He even liked Karpov while most of the female nurses hated him, and wanted him gone, sent to the back wards, sent up the hill to West Lawn. And he knew how to charm Bessie into somewhat reasonable behavior.

She had been looking at Paul over the chart rack, caught herself and shifted her eyes to Frieda. She didn't like the smell of cigarettes and thought it a stupid habit but conspired with the rest to ignore several of the nurses' transgressions.

Paul was attractive, and sensual, and called her doctor with European respect. Something had prevented her from asking him to call her by her first name but she would do this soon. They had been talking, gossiping, with Marjorie joining in occasionally as she wrote her notes. For some patients the progress note stumped her. She could think of nothing that was not banal, or empty. On Snow's chart she had noted his improved sleep, but also noted that there had been no change in his mood, or his willingness to talk about himself.

Frieda was saying something about Karpov being a royal pain in the ass and she didn't know why he was here. It was said to Paul but indirectly to Marjorie.

Paul said, "He's not so bad."

Frieda rolled her eyes and said, "Give me a break." And to Marjorie, "What are your plans for him?"

Marjorie looked up and said, "I don't think anyone makes plans for Mr. Karpov."

"Just what I was saying," said Frieda.

Marjorie looked at her watch and muttered, "Shit."

Paul was saying, "If you listen to him he has some very interesting things..."

"Bullshit as far as I can tell."

Marjorie said, "I'm late for my supervision with Dromore." She began to stuff the charts back in the rack.

Paul said, "Leave them. We have to go through them anyway."

She gathered her purse and a folder of notes and left the nurses' station. She was wearing a patterned matching top and skirt, long and full, belted at her hips, which she knew she could carry off very well with her height.

She left the ward and walked to the administration wing where Dromore had his office. She knocked on his door and then entered when she heard his voice.

He was sitting in his easy chair, sucking on his pipe, reading a journal held at arm's length. His reading glasses lay unused on his desk. He lifted himself out of the chair and moved behind the desk as he spoke, scattering ashes, then tamping down his pipe with a silver apparatus. "Well, what do we have today, Dr. Brennan?"

Marjorie chose a hardback chair and pulled it closer to the desk. Before answering she glanced at the journal Dromore had been reading. Acta Scandinavia. Very impressive. But maybe it contained summaries in English.

"They still haven't found Jeanie."

Dromore leaned forward and tapped out his pipe. "How long has it been now?"

"Five days."

"You're wondering if you should keep the bed open?"

"No. I'm worried about her."

"Is your charting up to date."

"Yes."

"Was she suicidal?'

"No. I didn't think so. I wasn't worried about her. But she's not a runner. I don't think she's ever eloped before."

"But she was quite delusional."

"I don't think she's acted on them. She never did in the past."

"It can still happen."

"I know. I have a bad feeling about this one."

"You can't save them all, Marjorie. She was a very pathetic creature, our Jeanie. It may have been a reasonable existential decision on her part, if she's dead I mean."

"I still feel bad. I talked with her the afternoon she disappeared. I didn't detect anything different. But I didn't give her much time."

"What about your other patients?"

She looked at him for a moment. He seemed not to want to talk about Jeanie anymore. She said, "I thought we might talk about depression." She put the folder on his desk, her purse on the floor.

"Ahh, Melancholia, Depression, and now Affective Disorder." He leaned forward and tapped out his pipe. "Melancholia is a fine old word. Pity we don't still use it. Of Cerberus and blackest midnight born. Black bile. Literally it means black bile. Have you read Burton's Anatomy? No? You should. I suppose 'Affective Disorder' reflects our knowledge of the chemistry of our moods but I do think it's a pity Melancholia has gone out of favor."

As he spoke Marjorie watched him fiddle with his pipe. He was perhaps 45 or 50 years old but he looked like a man who had always been 45 or 50. His speech, his manners, his dress, his affectations were those of someone who knew only maturity. And yet there was a baby-like innocence about his face, a certain femininity to his hands. He seemed to have leapt to midlife from childhood, bypassing adolescence and youth.

He was now talking of Churchill's dog days and Sylvia Plath's Bell Jar, his tone measured and scholarly as always. She thought how intimidated she had been early on in their association. How he could take the small, pitiful, personal struggle of one patient and relate it to the struggles of mankind through the ages, the great themes in poetry, philosophy, religion. She could easily feel overwhelmed and inadequate in his presence, returned to childhood, a stammering Dorothy before the Wizard.

She looked at the photos on the wall, his own teachers, and recognized a theme in Dromore's words. He was forging a great chain of being: Pinel, then Kraepelin, Bleuler, then Freud, then Dromore. To link his name with theirs he needed an audience of lesser scholars.

He paused to relight his pipe and Marjorie said, "There's one specific depressed patient I'd like to talk about. A new patient. Dr. Robert Snow."

"Doctor?"

"Turns out he's an internist from Toronto by way of Baltimore. A physician as well as an alcoholic as he puts it."

"And?"

"The police picked him up naked on the fire escape of a slum hotel on Water Street."

"Threatening to jump?"

"No, intoxicated, drugged up, just gazing about. But they found a suicide note in his room. I have it here somewhere." She took a piece of paper from her folder, handed it to Dromore. He read it quickly.

"Drunken ramblings, angry depressive tones. Incomplete, as if his energy failed. Most serious suicide notes are quite succinct and rational."

"So you don't think it was a serious attempt?"

"Angry thrashing about is more like it."

"Can I tell you about him?"

"Certainly, certainly. Start from the beginning." He leaned back in his chair, his slight paunch pulling at the buttons of his vest.

Marjorie told him what little she knew of Snow's story while Dromore alternately gazed out the window, played with his pipe and ran his fingers through his beard.

"He hasn't told you very much has he?"

"A family history of depression and alcoholism, some need to be rescued by a woman, this Jennifer in Baltimore, a sense of humor, estranged from his family, I suppose I should look into his licensing status."

"I should think that would be up to him."

"He doesn't seem interested at the moment."

"At least you have an intelligent patient for a change."

"He is that."

"He'll give you a run."

"He seems content to just sit it out for a while."

Dromore took a long drag and blew out slowly. The smell reminded Marjorie of sweetened cherries.

"Well, yes. This institution was once called an asylum."

"Pardon me?"

"I was just thinking of the original purpose for this building."

"This building?"

"Well, the others. Don't be so literal, Dr. Brennan. I presume you've started him on antidepressants?"

"Yes. Amitriptyline."

"And A.A.?"

"He's been a member."

"So you treat his depression and send him back to Toronto. It isn't up to us to sort out his whole life."

"No. I suppose not."
"And Marjorie, watch the transference with this one."

TWELVE

Walter Jabronski was tall, thin, and prematurely stooped. His pants were too big and the shoes he got from the shoe pile every morning never fit him well. His fingers were deeply nicotine stained, his shoes unlaced. His hands trembled from years of neuroleptic medication, his mouth chewed constantly, occasionally his cheek spasmed. His life had blended into the routines of the institution. He bummed coffee and cigarettes. He walked with a slow Modecate shuffle. He was not sane. Half thoughts flittered through his brain like drunken sparrows. Sometimes his brain was empty, sometimes mulling over a major injustice from 1968 when he lost his job as a bus driver. When you spoke to him he sometimes ignored you, sometimes focused momentarily. If you asked, "How are you today, Walter?" he might start his answer all right, with "fine", for instance, and then lose it in a sentence that dribbled away with references to his mother and Jesus. At least that's how Marjorie thought of him as he awaited transfer back to West Lawn after an unsuccessful two weeks in a boarding home and a readmission to West 3. Which was why she was so surprised to see him hurry onto West 3 after his walk on the grounds, come straight toward her and then tell his story clearly and in detail.

He had been shuffling along the path by the edge of the forest when he had to pee. Marjorie wondered for a moment why this posed such a big problem for Walter because he was known to simply pee in his pants when too preoccupied with voices or delusions to find a bathroom, and then walk around all day oblivious to the dampness and odour. This time, however, he didn't want to pee in his pants. He decided to make his way into the woods to find some privacy. He had to go a long way in. Every time he turned around he could still glimpse the upper floors of West Lawn. Finally deep enough to be hidden by the thick undergrowth he dropped his pants. He explained to Marjorie that the zipper wouldn't work, it never worked. He aimed his stream of urine at the trunk of a fallen birch tree, and as his water arced in the air, too late he realized the birch limb was a leg, a person.

He pulled his pants back up as fast as he could and pissed inside them. After all that.

The person didn't move. She was dead, he told Marjorie, dead, and it was that other patient. Jeanie? Asked Marjorie. Yes, Jeanie. She's got a rope around her. Around her neck? Asked Marjorie, her stomach in her throat as if feeling the hanging noose herself. Her neck and her legs, said Walter, and then, his story told, he asked Marjorie if he could have a smoke, and Jesus, Lord Jesus, would care if the flies came at night.

They found her where Walter had told them to look. Marjorie, Dr. Brennan, who had assisted at autopsies years before, threw up her lunch. Jeanie was a mess. An Exacto knife lay beside her naked body, with which she'd apparently tried to cut off her breasts, her small, unused, wasted breasts. And then she'd hung herself, horizontally, by tying one end of a cord to her neck and the other to a tree trunk and then rolling or falling down an embankment. Acting on a delusion, maybe, or a command hallucination, thought Marjorie. The flies had found her quickly and planted their eggs in her mouth, her nose, her eyes, her vagina. And then the rodents. Marjorie retched again, and then left the scene as the police arrived.

There was a deep hollow feeling in Marjorie's chest as she walked down the hill with Paul, but still she noticed, perhaps as such explicit contrast, the ocean cleansed sky, and the cumulus clouds riding the Pacific winds that felt so fine on her face. Paul said nothing until they were at the door of the building housing West 3. Without looking at her he said, "Her ankles were tied."

It took Marjorie a minute, so caught up was she in feeling responsible for Jeanie's suicide. She stopped and turned to Paul. "It might have been murder?"

"Jeanie wouldn't have done that to herself."

Marjorie was disgusted by her first reaction: relief. It might not have been her fault. She had no way of predicting and preventing murder. She hoped it was murder. Then empathy won out. Had it been suicide, at least it would have been in Jeanie's control, have been her decision. But mutilation and death by someone else's hand...She left Paul and sat alone in her office a good hour before driving home. Now she wanted Jeanie's death to be suicide, if she couldn't make it go away all together. Murder meant some incredibly sick sadistic bastard had been on the grounds of Essondale, might still be here.

Who the hell could do such a thing? A sadistic psychopath? It was just a label. It didn't help any.

The staff and patients on West 3 would know all about it by now, but they'd have to discuss it and announce Jeanie's death formally tomorrow. What had Dromore said to her the other day?" You can't save them all, Marjorie." And once before that, "We have our cancers too." It didn't help.

THIRTEEN

The ward was in an uproar. Dr. Brennan and the nurses had gathered all the patients in the day room to tell them Jeanie was dead. Two patients fled from the room in tears, nurses running after them. The psychotics got more psychotic. An older lady said it wasn't safe here anymore. Karpov said it was the fault of the staff, they weren't sufficiently vigilant. Hardy kicked a chair and strode from the room cursing. Some of the patients just sat there, not taking it in, not reacting. To Robert Snow sitting quietly in this group Marjorie Brennan looked quite shaken. Snow noticed the people, the events around him had taken on a sharper focus. He was no longer quite so overwhelmed by his own dilemma. Brennan and the nurses went back to their routines. Snow selected a chair along the wall of the dayroom. The television flickered in the far corner of the dayroom and its tinny voice assaulted the stale air. Some patients sat around it as if it were a hearth, watching, not watching. The patients smoked. They almost all smoked. They sat holding their tins of Imperial tobacco and their cigarette papers in their laps. Snow was part of this, part of this group, and yet alone. There had been a death. It meant very little to him. The gnawing emptiness in his chest meant more.

Karpov wheeled over to Snow, sat looking at him for a full minute, and then said, quite suddenly, "Kill me. Take this knife and kill me. You are a man who could do this. I have waited a long time for such a man. I know Robert Snow will understand."

Snow looked at him, said, "I don't understand."

Karpov's chair was right in front of Snow. He leaned forward, the knife retreating into his sleeve. "There is no life for me now. I have run from the communists, and before them the fascists. I have run from my family. I have run from the university. I have run from doctors and hospitals. My books have become false friends. I must die. Karpov must die. Take the knife."

Snow was held by Karpov's dark eyes. Then he turned his head to escape Karpov's breath. "Karpov, what the fuck is this all about? You're not happy here, why don't you leave?"

"This is not a place one can leave. There are no exits here. You don't see it yet do you? I created this place. I, Victor Karpov, I built this with my own hands."

"You're talking about your paralysis?"

"My legs have nothing to do with this. This is nothing." He slapped his thin, dead thigh. "Nothing compared to the deadness of my heart. That I have done myself. The drum is big, but empty. I do not have the courage to live any longer. Here, take the knife." He pushed the knife at Snow and Snow looked away.

"If you're so determined to die, Karpov, why don't you do it yourself?" He was surprised to hear the cruelty in his own voice.

"Aha, I thought I understood you. I have been wrong. You kill everything around you but finally you are afraid to kill Karpov. You are the coward, not I." Karpov withdrew the knife and reached for his tobacco pouch.

"This is crazy. This place is not conducive to good mental health."

"Who are you to judge what is crazy and what is not? What do you know of torment? What do you know of life? What do you know about madness? Nothing. Nothing. Nothing. I was wrong. I saw it in your eyes but I was wrong."

Karpov was breathing heavily. In the poor light of the dayroom, he bent to roll a cigarette. When he had struck a match and lit the cigarette, filling the space between them with blue smoke, he looked again directly at Snow, the cigarette cupped in his hand.

"It is a gift I offer you. A gift few men experience. The moment you kill me - even before - the moment you take this knife you will find freedom. It is the only true freedom."

"You're not making sense."

"I have taken a lot of trouble with this knife. For weeks I sharpen it. See what a fine point it has." With his free hand he again showed the knife to Snow.

"You have your books, Karpov, and your friends."

"Books. I tire of books. I tire of words. And without words Karpov is nothing. Words are nothing."

"Ah shit."

"What did you say?"

"I said shit, for Crissakes." Snow found his voice raised in anger.

"Then I will do it myself and join Jeanie in the great adventure," said Karpov, quickly wheeling away, and adding, his back now to Snow, "Later."

Snow stared after him and then looked through the high windows at the fading light. There was a strong wind moving the leaves of trees in the distance. It was then he remembered standing at the dormitory window and seeing a man and a woman far in the distance walking along the border of the forest and then disappearing within it. Jeanie and someone? That someone was not in a wheelchair. And there was no reason to believe that was Jeanie. But the couple walking reminded him of walking with Jennifer and years before that, with Ann.

They had been walking on the sidewalk by the houses on the cliff above the water. There was a small park ahead with large oak trees, grass, a dirt path. They could see the water from here and beyond the water the mountains rising to white peaks. The mountains were layered and went on forever. The water was alive with white sails. The city lay to their right, solid and square and clean. She reached up and touched the oak leaves as they passed under a large branch, and then twirled and held his arm.

"I'm so happy," she said. Her eyes contained a question.

She was beautiful and alive. There was energy in her movements and in her voice. He smiled at her and rested against the iron railing and looked down upon the beach below and out at the sails bunching and separating. She stood beside him and looked out the way he was looking, leaning against the railing.

"It scares me," she said.

He turned toward her and saw the fear in her eyes and didn't understand the reason for it and then understood the reason for it. She'd been right to question whether it would last, whether he'd fuck it up somehow.

The white sails below them were racing around buoys spread across the bay. There was a wind from off the Pacific that dwarfed the sails. The wind blew against the salt-bright light, and moved the leaves and blew against the city.

FOURTEEN

Dr. Brennan was distracted. She appeared nervous. She asked Snow about his sleep. He told her it was a little better, maybe he was waking at six rather than five. His appetite, what about his appetite? I'm eating, Snow told her. And your mood, has there been any improvement in you mood? Well, Snow began, and then fell silent. He didn't know. His chest was still hollow. There was still no humor. Maybe he felt something the other day. Mostly he was still dead wood, hollow, flat, eaten inside by termites, his cardiovascular system functioning, all his cells working, nothing much else, maybe a little yearning, and maybe it wasn't all depression, maybe he'd voluntarily shut down all systems, to avoid this life he'd created for himself. He didn't say this to Brennan. He thought it slowly to himself. She didn't seem to notice. She was saying, almost mechanically, "This is the dangerous period treating depression, you get some energy back but you still feel hopeless."

He said, "This Jeanie..."

She looked at him from behind her desk.

He said, "I seem to kill everything I have, everything good, not the way..."

"You have a depression, Dr. Snow. It makes you feel guilty about everything. It's an illness."

"It's a convenient explanation."

"So you want to punish yourself?"

He didn't answer.

"Okay, for what?"

"The people who love me, I put them through hell."

"Women?"

"All right, women."

"Why do you get so angry at...us?"

"I don't. I just close off. I go away. I desert them."

"This Jennifer?"

"Jesus, did I fuck up. There she was. Not asking much. Had to stay sober is all."

"And?"

"And I didn't."

"She was sweet, she was loving, she was competent, she offered herself to you and you puked all over her."

The vulgarity startled him. He began to say he didn't.

She said, smiling a little, "You paint yourself as an unmitigated bastard and then you work hard to deny it, and you work even harder at gaining forgiveness."

"Right."

"You want it from me?"

"I don't expect it."

"What then?"

"You're the doctor."

Later, walking on the grounds, he thought about her outburst. The ice-cold mistress of Essondale was not so ice-cold. She'd said, "This is fucking bullshit. Let me tell you something. Women are just people. You expect too much and you expect too little. Jeanie's lying in the morgue because someone didn't think she was human. Someone was disappointed. Someone was enraged. God almighty." Then she apologized and said it wasn't a good day. When his depression had lifted more they would talk again.

Before going for the walk on the grounds he wrote Jennifer a letter, and then his daughter Elizabeth. The letter to Jennifer was short. He wrote: Dear Jen, I won't ask anything of you now and I won't try to see you now & I don't blame you for not taking my calls. I'm in a treatment centre. All right. It's actually a psychiatric hospital. But I have to do this on my own. I have to get my head straightened out once and for all, and then, maybe then I'll ask you.

He wanted it in her hands now. He mailed it in the box outside the tuck shop and told himself it'll probably take a week, but what the hell is another week?

Brennan wasn't sure if she should be proud or ashamed of her outburst. It was a bad day. Two detectives had come to see her right after the ward meeting. What could she tell them? She told them Jeanie was a schizophrenic then switched that to a woman who had chronic schizophrenia, and that she was harmless. Relatives who visited? Boyfriends? Marjorie told them no one visited, maybe now and then she talked with some of the male patients, and a couple of times in the past some sexually aggressive male had taken advantage of her passivity, her naivety. They asked was she actively psychotic? Could she have done it to herself? She'd told them Jeanie was psychotic but hadn't done anything remotely like this in the past. One of them had stood staring out the window, the other asked her questions and took notes. They were RCMP they told her and Marjorie had been surprised by this but realized Mounties were seldom mounted these days. They weren't particularly big men like city cops seemed to be.

The one by the window had turned to say something about respecting patient confidentiality but do you know of any male patients currently in hospital who have done this kind of thing before, or any violence against the person? Marjorie had gotten defensive at first and told them, as well they should know, that the vast majority of psychiatric patients were victims, not perpetrators. Then she relented, thought for a minute and said no. Would she tell them if she thought of anyone? Marjorie said she would. She thought of, but didn't mention Matthew Hardy. On one of his admissions they'd found a sharpened machete in his duffle bag, and he was one of two males who had used Jeanie, had sex with Jeanie, giving her cigarettes or candy afterward. Jeanie never complained. In fact she was know to barter for extra cigarettes before the act. But the nurses had been upset. Jeanie wasn't. Christ. Who knows? Maybe he'd been good for her. There was a sweet side to him when he wasn't high.

She had asked them if it was definitely homicide. The older one closed his notebook and told her that would be up to the inquest to determine, but he'd seen stranger suicides. Hard to know. Brennan had said, "She didn't do it by herself." The image of Jeanie's body floated before her eyes. Stark white in places, mottled in others, dirt and leaves carelessly sticking to her, flies and some beetles moving on her, in and out, feeding on the cuts in her breasts.

When they had left she'd sat alone for a few minutes wondering why she'd come to work today. Addie was sniffling this morning when she dropped him off at the centre, stuffed up and producing thick guck when she blew his nose, leaving him in a room with all the other little darlings sniffling and hacking. You could see the bloody germs floating in the air. But it wouldn't have been a good day to stay home, give the wrong impression altogether, that she couldn't handle it. A suicide or a homicide. John's look had settled it. That concerned look on his face, that 'Adam really doesn't look well this morning' crap he was giving her, not once offering to do anything about it, forcing her to tell him the child was fine, when she wasn't so sure. Maybe John could pick him up. Don't be ridiculous. She could hear his answer already. Marge, any other afternoon, but we've still got a kidney to do, three, four hours. He'll probably get home around seven, whip out his stethoscope and play doctor on the kid. She had sighed to herself as she remembered she'd promised Dr. Snow she'd see him. Just what she needed now, spend an hour with a guilt-ridden depressed immobilized internist.

FIFTEEN

It was Karpov sitting on the balustrade two flights up, his useless legs dangling over the edge in the large open rotunda of the admission wing of Essondale. The floor was hard, patterned marble. A curving flight of steps led up to the second floor and then again to the third floor. Above Karpov the ceiling was domed.

Snow had heard the alarm as he walked back from the Tuck Shop, down the blacktop pathway to the back entrance of the admission building. The ringing alarm grew in volume as he entered the building and then abruptly stopped. A small crowd was standing in the centre of the rotunda looking up. Snow followed their gaze and there was Karpov perched on the edge. More patients arrived. No one seemed to know what to do. A lab-coated doctor was saying to a nurse, "How the hell did he get up there? I thought he was paraplegic."

"He can walk with two canes when he wants to."

"Christ, first we have a murder and now we have this."

"They're not saying it was murder."

"Yeah, no shit. She tied her feet up before she hung herself?"

"It's possible. Victor, come down from there."

"I am Karpov, my fine woman. Soon you will be able to say he was Karpov. Ah, Snow, I'm glad you could come to my little party." His voice was loud and resonant in the marble vault.

Snow imagined him crumpled on the hard floor below -white marble background, white coats, red blood, dark broken body.

"Perhaps I can fly," said Karpov. "Many things are possible."

"Victor, lean back and swing your legs over. I'm coming up to help." The nurse started up the wide curving steps but Karpov stopped her.

"Don't come near or you will see me fly sooner than you expect. No one come near me." He shifted his weight, sending a responsive quiver through Snow. "Is this not what Sartre would do, or Tolstoy, or Gorky? I am merely helping the hand of God a little. He will say, 'Why are you here so soon, Karpov?' And I will answer, 'It is not so soon. I have lived a lifetime. I have lived to see your grand design and I don't think much of it'. Heh, maybe God is a woman, Snow. How would you like that? Woman was born three days before the devil."

Snow noticed Melanie in the gathering crowd, her eyes riveted on Karpov. A vacant-faced young man shuffled by, stiff-legged, seemingly unaware of the Bulgarian and the crowd.

"This is not an important thing," shouted Karpov. Go about your business. You are ants, merely ants. Or molluscs, bipedal molluscs. Leave the area. I want no witnesses. All but you, Snow. You stay. You need to see a man fall to his death."

"Why are you doing this to me?" asked Snow.

"What was that, Mr. Snow?"

"I said why are you doing this?"

"Because you, Snow, you are a coward. You would not take my knife and kill me and you would not stop me. You would do nothing. We are not put here on this earth to do nothing, Snow. We are here to do something."

"What? Do what for God's sake?" His voice echoed like an answering chant.

"This is what I do," said Karpov. "Ich kann nichts anders."

"What?"

Anything. It doesn't matter. We all fertilize the soil in the end, as Jeanie will, when they finish butchering her. It doesn't matter what we do."

"What's the point of this?" asked Snow. It was almost said to himself but Karpov heard it in the sudden silence of the crowd.

Karpov responded in a quiet but audible voice, "The point is suffering. The point of Christian life is suffering. And I have no longer the capacity to suffer. It is time to try the last and greatest experiment. Think of it, Snow. In a moment I will know whether death can alter my existence, and my understanding of the world."

With a sudden crash the door on the second landing flew open. Hardy stood there for a moment staring upward at Karpov. A male nurse grabbed his arm. Hardy pulled himself free and then hit the nurse solidly in the face. As the nurse fell back against the wall Hardy dashed up the flight of stairs to Karpov. His Stetson rode on his shoulders. His bare tattooed arms grabbed Karpov and dragged him backward off the balustrade. Robert Snow stood open-mouthed for a moment, and then, vaguely exhilarated by Hardy's heroic rescue, and not knowing what else to do, resumed his journey to ward 3 West.

SIXTEEN

His bed was damp and hard. It screamed when he moved. The air was heavy with fear-sweat, ashes, damp wool and disinfectant. He lay on this bed thinking of the piss-stains and dribble hidden by the thin cotton sheets. A full moon illuminated the window bars and cast shadows across the lumps and bodies in other beds. The bodies lay as corpses, some face up, mouth open, others curled small in fetal position. Their breathing was ragged and harsh. A small stream of light flickered through the door and a shadowed figure entered, hesitated and then danced her light beam over each bed. Her intrusion caused moans, coughing, choking. She stepped back and disappeared.

In the far corner an old man sat up and stared ahead, then down, and picked at his blankets. His fingers worked, and worried, and picked at the blankets like a seamstress searching for a flaw. Snow was sweating and his heart pounded. He could hear it's heavy rapid pounding in his chest and in his ears. He knew it might stop unless he willed it to beat. This is one fuck of a place to die. But he knew the trick of accepting his fate, of ignoring his heart, of letting it do what it wants. His sweat was cold and he pulled the blanket over his shoulders. The pill began to do its work.

He drifted away and then jolted back, for a moment unsure whose bed he was in, which city, why. It seemed important to know which way was south. He drifted again and in his dream he was climbing a scaffold, high above the city. The scaffold wavered, slanted dangerously. He crawled onto the top layers of planks, lying flat, hanging on, afraid to stand up and trust the metal railing. He knew he once could fly, but not now, not in this dream. To climb down he had to swing his body over the edge and find the ladder with his feet. The planks shifted and tilted, swung back, tilted again. He was over the edge, his toes searching for the rungs, which were just out of reach. His nails dug into the soft wooden planks. Pieces came away in his hands. He started to fall as the solid structure crumbled. He knew this was a dream, and he shook his head to loosen the grip of sleep. It wouldn't clear. He was lying, falling, smothering behind his eyes. He made a final effort and his eyes opened, not yet seeing. He closed them. He could feel the pillow now, then his hands, and finally his feet. He rolled and touched something warm. A body, a female body. His mind made it Jennifer, the curve of her hip.

"Shhh."

"What?"

"It's me, Melanie."

"What are you..?"

"Hardy told me to come tonight."

"What?"

"To come to you. He said you needed me."

"Jesus. I mean what..."

"I'll go if you don't want me."

"But Christ. You can't..." He made no further protest. She moved down under the covers, stroking, feeling, licking, rubbing all over. He felt her small buttocks. He grasped her thighs, and placed a hand on her damp sparse curls. Her odour was animal, pungent, urgent, of adolescent sweat and sweet perfume. He had an erection in spite of my fear and confusion.

"You're doing fine," she said.

He came in silence, with her mouth prolonging the spasm, and then lay still, drawing his hands away quickly. She slipped naked from under the sheet and he saw her silhouetted in the light from the door. I want her to stay but she wrapped a blanket around herself and tiptoed away, paused at the door, looked back briefly, then disappeared. He slept peacefully through the rest of the night.

SEVENTEEN

Rain billowed up the Fraser River Valley. The dark clouds hung heavily close to the road and cut off the mountains on either side. The telephone poles were blackened on their western side and trees bent before the gusts of wind.

She drove against the rain, down the Fraser Valley. It was damp and close inside the car. The windows had misted with her first few breaths. Her umbrella dripped a puddle on the newspapers, receipts and candy wrappers littering the floor. She would be late today, late picking up Adam, late getting to the Safeway, late fixing a meal. She had left the building behind but Essondale refused to vacate her mind. Christ. Hardy in seclusion after hitting a nurse. Melanie cutting her wrists after a session with Dromore. Karpov on one-to-one. Dr. Robert Snow just sitting there day after day. Christ, depressives. She should have told the cops about Hardy. The image of Jeanie's corpse made her shiver. It was the gossip of Essondale. The staff loved this sort of shit. No, that's not fair. The nurses who knew Jeanie were grieving. A lot of them would go to her funeral. Melanie, the place was making her sicker. She'd wanted to discharge her but Dromore had quoted something about regression in the service of the ego or some shit and insisted that she was much to sick, her only hope was a constant infusion of ego strength, keep her from fragmenting. Maybe. Shit knows. She should have mentioned Hardy to the cops.

She heard the muffler rattle as her old Toyota hit a bump on the approach to the Lougheed Highway. The mess in her car annoyed her as it always did on wet, cold days. She resolved, once again, to clean it out on the first sunny weekend.

Normally she could reach the day care centre on the east fringe of Vancouver by five-thirty, pick up her two year old, stop at the nearest grocery, buy something for supper and get home to their 16th Avenue apartment by 6:15, in time to clean up a bit and begin supper before John arrived. But the traffic was moving slowly through the rain, feeling its way through the mist clouds that hung low in the Valley. The left hand wiper was missing a spot just at eye level and the

65

defroster couldn't keep up with condensation. Marjorie wound her window down a crack and wiped at the windshield with a piece of Kleenex. She had to hunch over the steering wheel to get a good view of the road ahead. She pulled her cardigan tightly around her neck and wound the window back up. The air was too humid to make much difference. She reached for the heater control, turned it down a notch and settled back for the long cautious drive. A line of cars and trucks accumulated ahead and she used their taillights as beacons to follow. The wipers flicked hypnotically across the glistening reddened windshield.

Last Sunday she had sat on a log beyond Kitsilano beach watching Addie dig in the sand, and watching the tide ripple around the sandbanks. He played in the mouth of a small stream that trickled through the sand. A man with pants rolled up to his knees walked by and smiled at them. The large white city sat at the end of the inlet to the east. There was always a wind, a cool wind that brushed against her sun-warmed skin. The sky was open and the mountains distant. The beach stretched away for miles on both her right and on her left. Hundreds of people sat and strolled and played and swam. Farther out she knew there was a beach for nude sunbathing, at the base of a cliff, where people built temporary shelters with logs and blankets that always flapped in the winds. She bent down and dug with Addie for a minute and then picked him up when he toddled away. She rinsed his hands in the stream and wiped the sand out of the corners of his mouth. The sun was hot and the wind was cool and on this beach where she should have been happy she wasn't.

She made another effort to wipe away the condensation on the windscreen, and pushed the squirter button to see if that would make a difference. The traffic in her lane slowed to a crawl. She considered the passing lane but thought better of it. Her hands were cold and she held each in turn under her cardigan to warm.

John would be writing his fellowship in anaesthesiology this November and for the remainder of his life making a living putting people to sleep. She had trouble understanding how such an activity could sustain anybody. Especially somebody like John with his sense of humour, his interest and enthusiasm and she wondered why she was giving him this testimonial as she drove through the rain to pick up their child and make his supper. He is a sweet man and a bloody rock and maybe the only thing that keeps her from fragmenting all

66

over the place. Maybe. Shit. Make his supper, wait on him, wait for him, mother him, look after his child, what the hell was she getting out of this? Last Sunday she was lonely, plain lonely. For all intents and purposes she was a single mother.

Just ahead where the feeder lanes from Richmond joined the main highway, traffic slowed and stopped. The rain had lessened now, but she wasn't able to see the cause of the congestion until she had inched forward another hundred yards. In the ditch at the side of the road a blue sedan lay on its side, glass shattered around it, the driver's door pulled off its hinges. A cop in a yellow slicker waved the traffic around as a tow truck grappled with the upturned vehicle. Two small groups huddled in cars parked on the shoulder as an ambulance pulled away from the scene. She had a flash in her mind that the car belonged to the day centre, returning from an excursion, Adam in the ambulance. She steadied herself.

She had spoken to George Guscott today about Melanie and had come off the phone wondering how intelligent men can be so thick when it came to pretty young girls. He was smooth though, his slick silver hair and his grey eyes boring into you. She had, after all, invited him up to her room at the conference last fall. To see the view she had said. Ah, well. It hadn't really mattered what excuse she had given. Her room did have a view and, bless his heart, he had looked at it first. He was on top of her on the bed, fully clothed, before she changed her mind and begged off. Changed her mind. She hadn't made it up in the first place. She gave him some excuse about being sore and tired and still nursing Adam, and apologizing, because she felt it was unfair to him. Unfair to him to come up 27 stories by elevator, feign interest in the Toronto skyline, and not get laid. Ahh, Marjorie, when will you ever decide what you want?

Her mother would have a nice phrase to cover it, something like making your bed and lying in it. Her life had never had possibility, even the thought of possibility. In the late afternoon Marjorie would, as a child, help her mother in the kitchen, and then as it grew dark and late, watch the road from the window in the dining area, the breakfast nook they called it, watching the headlights, trying to guess which belonged to her father's car. They were all different and she would know immediately which was his unless she watched too closely. Her mother worried about her father and why he was late, and often glanced out the other window above the sink. In her mother's anxiety

Marjorie imagined accidents, ambulances, police phoning. The
Everware pots on the stove boiled the vegetables, boiled them
tasteless, and the oven baked a meat loaf or shepherd's pie. Each
night her mother's anxiety raised Marjorie's' hope. Mother was
worried about him. She wanted him home tonight. Which meant,
Marjorie reasoned, that when he finally came in the door she would
be grateful to see him, and kind, and pleasant, and they and her two
brothers, who had been drifting through the kitchen and hunting in the
refrigerator, would sit down for a nice family dinner. Not bloody
likely. Shit. She would start on him the moment he walked in the
door, and keep it up throughout the meal. And he would sigh and ask
if, just this once, they might have a peaceful meal, and couldn't she
say something pleasant for a change, which contained it's own
nastiness of course, and then her brothers, on cue, sensing, no doubt,
how close they were to their parents' flashpoint, would start a fight
between themselves.

Years later, after many not so peaceful and not so pleasant family
dinners, her father had stood by the kitchen sink, on a weekend, and
announced that he was leaving. It was, he said, his last chance for
happiness. He had made a move. He had exercised a possibility.

Thinking about this Marjorie almost missed her exit ramp. When
she caught herself and swung off she felt a moment's regret leaving
behind the small amount of time she could have alone. She reached
down and turned on her radio to a pre-set FM station. It was choral
music she didn't recognize. The rain had been easing and now the
drizzle stopped. The sky quickly opened in the west to a brilliant sun
embroidering the water-laden clouds with shades of pink and violet. It
often happened in the late afternoon, as if God were apologising for a
day of rain. Marjorie accepted the apology and wished she had time
and a place to stop and enjoy it. But off the highway she had to
concentrate on her driving in the rush hour traffic.

She pulled into the parking lot of the day-care centre and sat for a
moment in her car. Five to six. Almost late. She needed a minute to
take a breath and shift her mind and her concerns from herself to her
child, her family. She knew it was best to take the minute. There was
a trick to it. She conjured images of Adam, alone, sweet, waiting with
a scribble to show her, offering his unconditional love. She pictured
his innocence, his vulnerability, and suddenly any reluctance she had
about fetching a tired, demanding, whining, sniffling child would

vanish and she would yearn to gather him up. Then she stepped out of the car and walked through the gate to find him playing, splashing in the puddles in his oversize Wellingtons, chasing the round-about, waiting for his mother.

That night she slept poorly. Images of chaos on the ward, Jeanie's mutilated corpse and a pervasive sense of shame fluttered behind her eyes.

She awoke from a dream, rolled over to touch John but remembered he was on duty at the hospital that night. She lay awake for a while, then got up to check on Adam. He was sleeping peacefully, sweetly in his small bed in his room with stuffed bears and a half dozen Fisher Price toys, colorful moving things hanging from the ceiling. Back in bed she was cold, and she wished for a body to spoon. She thought of bringing Adam to bed with her, felt like bringing Adam to bed with her. She got up again, pulled on her dressing gown, looked at Adam, and then padded out to the kitchen.

She hunted through the cupboards and refrigerator for something that might be satisfying. She knew she wouldn't find what she really wanted in either place. A bowl of cereal would have to do. She filled a bowl with honey coated flakes, topped it with some maple syrup and covered it with half and half, moitie et moitie she read on the carton. Christ. Fat city. She diluted the cream with some 2%. She sat at the kitchen table looking out over the lights of Vancouver, a glorious, hedonistic, fun loving city, climbing up the southern slopes of the Coastal Range. A wonderful place with the highest suicide rate in Canada.

Her mother had been hospitalised twice before she lay on the bed she had once shared with her husband and held the plastic bag over her head. It was a large freezer bag Marjorie remembered, a zip lock bag. Shit. An overdose would have been easier to handle. She didn't need that image floating around inside her skull every day for the rest of her life. Her father was fit and tanned and remarried. She had not forgiven him. Obviously. She had even forgotten his birthday, not just one year, but the actual date of his birth. He had made his choice and she imagined he lived inside it. Her mother had spent three years sleeping on the sofa by the television, the television always on, a cigarette always burning. It had been late for her to learn to live alone. Except for that one time, just recently out of hospital. She had phoned and talked and said that she had discovered the real problem was not

learning to live with someone else but learning to live with yourself.
If you could live with yourself you could live with almost anyone.
She was, she said, learning to live with herself. Maybe she could
travel, make new friends. Insight, thought Marjorie as she finished the
last of the bowl of too-sweet cereal, is a highly over-rated commodity.

Adam was crying. She walked back to his room. Through the
window she could see that the sky above the mountains was flickering
with the first blush of dawn.

EIGHTEEN

"Hardy's in seclusion." Karpov said it in a whisper through a mouthful of scrambled eggs at breakfast. Close by an aide sat watching Karpov, still on one-to-one.

"Why seclusion?" asked Snow.

"He hit a nurse."

"That's true."

"So there he is, locked in a bubble room, a mattress on the floor, bread and water rations. The birthright of every revolutionary."

"Karpov, he's not a revolutionary. He's just a boy - a sick boy. He rescued you for Chris' sake."

"I know, I know, Robert. But we all must have our dreams, eh?" He grinned at Snow, showing his bad teeth. "Ah yes, I forgot, you have no dreams. Tell me, Robert, did you ever have dreams?"

"I'm going back to see Hardy."

"They won't let you see him."

Snow ignored Karpov, picked up his tray and made his way past the depressives, the schizophrenics, the chronics, the faces of despair, confusion, resignation, apathy, and suspicion, down the long pathway between tables, over to the return trolley. He lined up behind a young man with a twisted face and a right arm he couldn't quite control. He waited while the man struggled to slip his tray into the rack and then placed his own in the slot above and left the cafeteria. He didn't know why he needed to see Hardy. What did the boy mean to him?

The nurse, Paul, sat outside the door of Hardy's seclusion room reading a newspaper. Snow found he was not interested in news from the outside world. Paul looked up. Snow said, "Could I see Hardy, talk to him for a minute?"

"How are you doing, Dr. Snow?

"I'd like to see Hardy."

"Well, Dr. Brennan's ordered no visitors and low stimulation. He got a little high when we..." He tapped the clipboard on his lap.

Snow waited. Paul folded his paper, got up from his chair and said, "Here, take a quick look through the glass if you want. Don't try to talk with him."

Snow put his face against the concave portal. The image was distorted, the floor and ceiling curved, pulling the corners of the room within his field of vision. Hardy, bent with the floor, lay naked on a soiled mattress, a single sheet twisted around the lower half of his body. His left arm and leg were spilled on the floor, his mouth open, yellowed spittle or blood on his chin, white crusts in the corners of his mouth. He looked dead but for the movement of his chest.

Snow walked away without looking at Paul, feeling small, powerless, insect-like. He hid the remainder of the day, sitting deep in an armchair in the dayroom. He watched the corridor through the door. He refused O.T. and the organized walk on the grounds. During the afternoon a student nurse tried to engage him in conversation and later another tried to entice him with a jigsaw puzzle. He felt he was losing his past, becoming an institutional dement. He sat silently, enduring their presence until each left in turn, he guessed, to write a report on his flat affect, his resistance, his uncooperativeness, his failure to socialize.

His watch was twice rewarded when Hardy was led from the seclusion room to the washroom, an aide on each arm. He could hear Hardy's grunts and slurred profanities and once he saw Hardy pull his arm away. He was somehow vaguely heartened by these gestures. Every hour a nurse arrived with syringe and vial and entered the room accompanied by at least two male aides or nurses. By mid afternoon, she came only once every two hours and Snow knew the first part of Hardy's ordeal was over. He was immobilized by this, waiting, watching. He wasn't sure what it had to do with himself, except Hardy was someone who just took from life, simply lived it as it happened, and he, Dr. Failed Snow, had some lessons to learn. Of course Hardy was nuts too, but what the hell? Jennifer would like the way Hardy just got on with it, jumped in with both feet, damn the consequences, nothing ventured, all that horseshit.

In the late afternoon Snow was called to Dr. Brennan's office.

"I understand you're not talking today." She put the chart down, arranged herself carefully in the chair, folded her hands in her lap.

Snow had trouble disliking her. It was the sadness in her eyes that appealed to him.

"Why do you have Hardy locked up?" he asked.

"Oh," she said, "is that the trouble? Do you have a special relationship with Mr. Hardy?"

"No," he answered quickly, annoyed to find a simple question turned back on him this way. "He seems to be the only person in this place with an unbroken spirit, that's all. And he was kind to me. He rescued Karpov."

"I can't really talk about another patient, Dr. Snow."

"I hate to see him drooling and staggering. Maybe you're giving him too much Haldol."

She raised her eyebrows. "Do you have opinions about my other patients?"

"No."

"No, really, I'd like to hear your ideas."

"I'm sorry. I'll keep out of it."

"Well, look. I'm a little touchy these days."

"Just that the kid was trying to get to Karpov."

"I understand. But he hit a nurse. What can I do? I've got to get him under control."

"You mean punished."

"No, I don't mean punished. And you said something about staying out of it."

"All right."

She looked at him for a moment. "Well, I'll tell you this much. He was manic and dangerous when they brought him in last time. We found a machete in his duffel bag."

Snow took a moment to absorb this. "I imagine he was frightened. He probably arms himself when he's frightened."

"That may be true, but a machete isn't a toy." Brennan paused. She seemed to be thinking.

Snow said, "Have they figured what happened to this person, Jeanie?"

Brennan looked at him. "Why do you want to know?"

"I don't know. This is all..." He shrugged, unsure why he'd asked.

"They've decided it was murder, or probable homicide was the way they phrased it. And she was mutilated with an Exacto knife they think came from one of our workshops. Anything else you'd like to know?"

"Am I still involuntary?"

"Yes."

"For how long?"

"Until you find a way of convincing me you're not going back to a hotel to kill yourself."

"How about drinking myself to death?"

"Drinking's okay. You can kill yourself slowly, that's your own problem. Only if you do it fast it's my problem. Besides, I'm not up to another death right now."

"For a moment there I thought you cared."

"Careful, Dr. Snow, you're smiling."

NINETEEN

Dromore gulped the last of his brandy and soda and took himself up to the bedroom he shared with his wife of 26 years. She was asleep on her side. When he crawled in beside her he turned his head away from her breath, which was acrid from wine and cigarettes. For years it had been mostly like this. She'd smoke and drink and take herself to bed early. He'd stay up and watch, God help himself, very bad television for another hour or two and read magazines, journals, novels, at the same time, until his eyes were sore and his body itched from inactivity. In bed he would read, and then lie awake thinking. Years before he would reach out and touch her, stroke her and she would roll away and remove his hand, or sweetly ask him to rub her thigh, which, to his unending consternation, meant just and only that. A thigh rub, an ass rub, God help us.

Now and again she would stop fighting him and release some passion in the middle of the night and he'd find himself wonderfully on top, on top and inside a writhing, moaning, loving thing, a woman he loved again, and this would give him power, power to hold an erection, to control an erection, on his knees and hands, his arms outstretched, his fingers entwined in hers, thrusting powerfully, thick and heavy, alive, and beating age and death once more.

What could he do? Leave her? How? Where? Why? Jesus. She'd... what would she do? No longer Mrs. Dr. Dromore. On her own in an apartment. Christ. She would make him pay. He would make him pay. The kids would make him pay. He was just not ruthless enough. Or was that all self-justifying bullshit? Probably. This rut he was in was comfortable, in a soul destroying way.

There was a definite inequality here. He walks, they gather around her and say, "Oh, poor woman, what a bastard he turned out to be." And if he takes up with a younger woman they gather around her and say, "See, what a foolish old man." But if she walks they gather around and say, "It's about time. We don't know how you stood it for so many years. Good for you." And if she takes up with a younger man, they gather around and say, "Well now, isn't that something. The best of luck to her."

His anger, at times, was so strong, so palpable, at least privately. He was sure it didn't show to others. He was at the height of his powers, he understood people so well, and, God, he was good, knowing what was best for these weak creatures. But he would have to stop what he was doing with Melanie. A couple of his private patients was one thing but this Melanie in the hospital was professional suicide. And maybe. And maybe he wanted that. No. He'd have to stop. No matter how much she needed it, how much she thrived on it. Like the others. God, how they blossomed under his direction, such poor, fragmented egos, psychotic without the infusion of his strength, regressive, but living fully because of what he could do for them. It was all true but it wasn't. He knew he used them for his own needs. But they were adults, weren't they? They could stop seeing him if they wanted to. They made choices.

But others wouldn't see it that way. He wasn't dumb. He understood the shame that would be heaped upon him if...if, Christ, he didn't like to think about it. If...if one of them complained, wrote a letter to the College, which they wouldn't do because they loved him and depended on him...but if one of them did...and maybe it was that danger that kept him at it, making it so erotic...what was sex without danger? An oyster without Tabasco.

They would ask him how he could do this thing, if he admitted to it, if they believed these unbelievable women, they would wonder how he could carry on this way at such a risk, him, one of the wisest, smartest men in his profession, should be acclaimed internationally if it weren't for the small minded bastards everywhere, the small minded bastards who didn't understand Cameron and Reich, "Listen, Little Man." Ah, yes. Even if Reich went nuts in the end with his Orgone box. Probably driven nuts by the small minded bastards. Still, and when he let himself worry like this he broke out in a flush, still, he was doing something that the little men would not think right and they'd get him, the bastards, and so he should stop, especially Melanie, and they'd all wonder how he could be doing such a thing, how he could psychologically bring himself to do it and live with it, but he understood from the many times he'd interviewed sex offenders and bank robbers, and from that patient who'd sit naked in her room and when you entered she'd deliberately take the index finger of her

76

left hand and reach behind and stick it up her anus and then slowly, carefully bring it back up in front and stick it in her mouth and lick it, all the time her eyes fixed on you, and everbody'd argue was it psychosis or not, because, Christ, how could anyone do that kind of thing if she wasn't crazy? And he knew the answer to that one, with robbing a bank, licking your own shit, doing what he was doing, maybe even murdering someone, the answer was, it's easy, at least after the first time. Only the first time is hard. Only the first time was hard. That's how he got into it. And now he couldn't stop. They wanted it. They expected it. No more, he'd say to himself, and then he was doing it again, because they needed it. And what a privilege for each of them, to have him, to please him, to know what it was like to be the subject of a priest-king.

TWENTY

"You know," said Snow, "this isn't so bad. Where's the snake pit and the cuckoo's nest?" He was pushing Karpov in his wheelchair along the blacktop path behind the admitting wing of Essondale.

"It's here, Robert, if you want to find it."

"The other buildings?"

"No, that is not quite what I mean, my dear innocent Robert."

"Well, what do you mean?"

"I think you're disappointed in this establishment, Robert. Perhaps you'd prefer Bedlam and Big Nurse to our Dr. Brennan and her poultices."

Snow stopped the wheelchair and gazed up at the glowering brick facade of West Lawn.

"If you listen closely," said Karpov, sensing the direction of Snow's gaze, "you can hear them moaning softly, keening for lost souls."

Snow listened to the distant traffic and the call of ravens from the forest high above the buildings. "It's just your imagination, Victor."

"Ah, but you are curious are you not? You wanted to see for yourself. In fact, you are the true romantic, Robert. You have an urge to throw yourself into the inferno, to be lashed and beaten and punished for your sins. I suspect it is a sin you have not even committed." He looked up at Snow. "Robert, my friend, you cannot be punished for a sin you have not committed. To sin you have to believe in something. You don't believe in anything, ergo you cannot sin and ergo you cannot be punished. Not by others at least. And when you punish yourself, Robert, it is a feeble, unsatisfying thing. There is no righteousness in it."

Snow gave the wheelchair a push and they resumed their journey.

"A lunatic asylum should be a lunatic asylum."

"It is," said Karpov, "it is. You are simply too blind to see it. It is all very subtle now. They have become much more clever in their ways."

"They? You're sounding paranoid."

"Of course I'm paranoid. Is it not sane and normal to be paranoid today? How else can one make sense of anything?"

"Good question."

"You'll see. This cannot all be accidental, a cosmic accident. It must be the design of a diabolical mind."

They went a little farther in silence and then Karpov said, "Robert, you have gotten where you are now by standing still. But if you want to see the inside of hell you must do something. Standing still won't get you into that building." He gestured with his cigarette toward West Lawn. "You must do something, anything. Perhaps if you had killed me when I asked, you would be in there now, chained to the wall like a mad beast, and finally satisfied."

"That's not what I want," said Snow. But he wondered. The drift downward was more alluring than a long tedious climb up. It had always been so. A small step to the complete and utter comfort of total failure. "Maybe. God knows."

"But God doesn't know, Robert."

Snow looked at Karpov flourishing his cigarette at the heavens, the sombre windows of West Lawn, two seagulls squawking and fighting over some litter by the Tuck shop, a young man walking by in unlaced pink jogging shoes, and he chuckled, and then he laughed.

"I have not seen you laugh before, Robert. You must be careful. Someone might see this and send you away."

TWENTY-ONE

Hardy was released from the bubble room and returned to his bed in the dormitory. After breakfast and medication Snow went back to see him. Jeanie's death was buzzing around again. It had quieted down for few days and then the rumours began again. Snow wondered how the patients got to know all this shit. The Exacto knife from the O.T. department, the rope from Industrial Therapy, the cops pissed because the area was trampled, her clothes spread around but they hadn't found her panties, but nobody really sure she'd been wearing any. The suspects included some escaped sex offender from the B.C. Pen just up the highway, or one of the patients right here. And they knew about Hardy's machete and some other time he busted up the dormitory and held everyone at bay with a knife. And Snow was getting interested, shit, at least it kept him from thinking about himself and his own fucked up life. And worrying whether Jen got his letter or not and why she hadn't written back or flown out. Flown out? Christ. Still living with fantasies. Take charge of his own life. Besides, he was feeling a little better, little more energy, these antidepressant pills doing their thing.

In the dormitory Hardy was sitting on the edge of his bed, shoulders slumped in a ratty hospital robe, his brown Stetson once again riding the back of his head.

Snow sat down on the bed next to Hardy's, said, "How you feeling?"

Hardy looked up. His face was a battleground of contrasts. His mouth was slack, crust in the corners, drool on his chin. His eyelids drooped heavily; his skin looked numb and lifeless and yet, in his eyes...in his eyes there remained a spark of defiance. When Hardy answered, his voice gargled from the back of his throat. "I'm alrigh' ...gimme smo, wou ya? Chris', they gaw me tawgin' li' a baby."

"You can't smoke in the dormitory," said Snow.

"The fug I can'. I'll smo' where I fuggin' well please." But he made no move to get a cigarette.

"They got you on some pretty heavy shit."

"You fuggin' go' tha' right."

"Have the police talked to you?"

Hardy didn't blink. "Fuggin' cops. Gaw nothin' better'n do'n swy on me. Fuggin' needle. Fuggin' pills. They c'n tay their fuggin' pills and shove'em. Gimme smo'."

"I don't have any."

A nurse appeared in the doorway and announced quite buoyantly, "Time for your pills, Matthew."

Without complaint Hardy took the white pills offered him and clumsily placed them on his tongue. Snow was going to say, Christ, he's already a goddamn cauliflower, but bit his tongue. Hardy took the paper cup of water and washed the pills down, swallowing visibly, head back, larynx bouncing up and down.

"That's my good boy," said the nurse.

Hardy waited until she had left the room and then he slowly, deliberately winked at Snow and stuck out his coated and tremulous tongue. On the tip were two white tablets.

"You'll have to show me how to do that," said Snow.

"Nothin' to it," said Hardy, spitting the pills into his hand. He got up and walked unsteadily to the washroom.   Snow waited. He heard a toilet flush and then Hardy reappeared. He collapsed back on his bed.

"I gotta ge' the fug outa here," he said.

"You can't go now," said Snow. "You can't even walk."

"Sure, sure, in a day or two, couple days maybe." He lay back on his bed and seemed to drift away from Snow.
Snow sat for a moment unsure what to do or say next. He had, although he was puzzled by it, a wish to help Hardy. But he didn't know how, and the very thought of helping someone else filled him with a sense of dread. He was such a shithole himself what right did he have even thinking about it. Help Hardy with what? Help him escape? Help him take his pills and be a good patient?

There was a gentle boy hidden somewhere inside this drugged and angry body.

"Can I get you anything?" he asked.

"Hmmmmph."

Snow left then, his questions unanswered.

"Come on, come on, come on, wake up. Ya gotta help me."

A hand was shaking Snow's shoulder as he startled and then pulled from his drug-aided sleep. It was Hardy. He'd been out of seclusion two days now and it was the middle of the night. Snow managed, "What? What?" as he propped himself on his elbows.

"I gotta get outa here."

"What are you talking about?"

"Man, I gotta get outa here."

"It's, Christ, it's three A.M. Why now?"

"Brennan told me. The cops are coming tomorrow to talk with me about Jeanie."

"So?"

"They'll pin it on me."

"Did you do it?"

"No. For Chris' sakes."

Karpov was sitting up in his bed now, watching them. The rest snored on.

"How can I help now, this time of night?"

"I need some clothes."

Karpov was pulling his legs over the edge of his bed and manoeuvring his wheelchair into position. " He said, "The door'll be locked, Matthew."

"I'll need the key. Come on, Dr. Snow, what about some clothes?"

"You should stay and talk to the police."

"Man, I can't do it."

Karpov pulled himself into his wheelchair. "Come, Robert, we'll get him clothes and run interference for him, like your football."

"Karpov, you'll get the boy killed."

"Killed? Is this better than death?" said Karpov, "A life in chemical restraints, a life without passion, a life with no pleasures?"

"Christ. He's innocent, he talks with the police, nothing happens."

"They'll pin it on him, Robert. They need a victim."

"You're talking shit," said Snow. "You're going to get the boy killed. You want him to do what you can't do yourself, escape, run, - the things you talk about but don't have the courage to do."

"I did it with Jeanie once," said Hardy.

The others were waking now, disturbed by the voices growing louder, rolling, groaning, coughing.

"What is it? What is it?" said the old man. "Is that you, Henry?"

"They've come to steal the moonbeam," said the gaunt young man.

"Steal," said the old man. "All my things have been stolen - all my pretty things."

"So?" asked Snow.

Karpov answered, "So everyone knows, including Brennan."

"That's still no reason to run."

"Give him your clothes, Robert, that's all he needs."

Snow settled back for a minute. Then he said, resigned, "Go ahead, take them." Why not?

Hardy stripped off his institutional pyjamas and grabbed Snow's pants, shirt, and underpants off the chair by the bed and struggled into them. Snow flinched at his used underpants being worn by another man but Hardy didn't seem to care.

Karpov wheeled his chair over between the beds and fetched Hardy's boots. Hardy was tucking in Snow's shirt when Karpov handed him his boots.

"My hat," said Hardy. "I need my hat." Karpov wheeled back and found Hardy's Stetson.

"All we need now is a horse," said Snow.

Hardy glowered at him.

"He made a joke," said Karpov. "The man made a joke. Forgive his impertinence. Here you are. Ah yes, what a vision. But we must be fast." He wheeled to the door, looked out, and turned. "There's a nurse at the door and she's locked it again."

"What about the window?" asked Hardy.

"Too small, too small. Have you any ideas, Robert?"

The others in the dorm were silent now, watching the three conspirators.

"How about the laundry chute?" said Snow. "We could send him down the laundry chute." He thought he was being ironic but Karpov responded as if it were a serious suggestion.

"Not a bad idea, Robert. I know you are a man of imagination all along. If it does not kill crazy Jane it certainly does not kill Tom Mix. I will distract the nurse at the end of the corridor, and you take Hardy across the hall to the chute. You should find it behind that false cupboard front."

"You're sure you want to do this, Matthew?"

"Of course he does. Of course he does," said Karpov.

"Let the boy answer for himself."

"I gotta get outta here, man."

"Okay," said Snow. He pulled himself out of his bed.

Karpov wheeled around the corner of the dormitory door and pushed at top speed toward the end of the corridor. Snow watched from the doorway.

When he reached the nurse, Karpov clutched his chest, looked to the ceiling and uttered a groan of fraudulent agony. Then he crumpled from the wheelchair and sprawled at the nurse's feet. She immediately knelt over him and rolled him on his back. Snow was startled to see what she did next and he imagined it came as a surprise to Karpov. She shouted, "Annie, Annie, Annie." and slapped Karpov twice across the face. Then she hiked her skirt, straddled his abdomen and gave him a resounding thump on the chest with a heavy fist. Karpov may have groaned, he may have moved, he may have gasped but the nurse was in position now, arms out-stretched, the heel of her left hand firmly planted on Karpov's lower sternum, the heel of her right hand on top of her left, pumping rhythmically up and down, counting one and two, and three.

Snow took Hardy by the elbow and led him across the corridor to the cabinet door on the wall. It was locked but he could easily get his fingers under the door. Hardy nudged him aside, put his fingers under the edge, pulled, leaned back. It came easily, the wood screws pulling out. Underneath was a hole in the wall about eighteen inches square.

He didn't have to help Hardy. The cowboy grasped the top of the cabinet with both hands and swung his legs up and into the opening. He looked at Snow, and then he let
go. His Stetson fell to the floor, too big for the laundry chute, but the rest of Matthew Hardy disappeared from sight.

There was a flurry of activity around Karpov at the end of the corridor. A loud speaker announced a code 99. The doors would soon open and more than sufficient staff would enter on the run and mill about. Nothing he could do. He returned to the dormitory thinking about how quickly he had gotten into something best avoided and how slowly he approached the solutions, maybe the possible solutions, to his own life.

TWENTY-TWO

Karpov and Snow were sent "up the hill." They were transferred to West Lawn. Karpov was still mending in the infirmary, recovering from the excessive ministrations of the enthusiastic night nurse recently certified in CPR. Karpov explained this to Snow later. "Christ," he said. "They practice on these plastic Resuci-Annies, jump right in there full force. She cracked two ribs." His actual transfer would have to wait. Brennan told Snow he was going.

"Dromore ordered it," she told him. She waited for a response. Getting none she stood up, paced, and said, "For God's sake, Dr. Robert Snow, M.D., FRCP, do you want to go up there? Talk to me. Say you're better. Tell me you're no longer suicidal, you want to be made voluntary and discharged. You're going back to Baltimore or Toronto. You'll attend A.A. Lie to me." She stood facing him, leaning against the wall, arms crossed. Her pose was more elegant than intimidating.

When Dromore had told her she'd said, "WHAT! ROBERT SNOW?"

He'd smiled at her reaction, then said softly, reassuringly, "Relax. This may just do it for him. He's going nowhere now. A week on West Lawn he just might decide to get better."

Karpov was another matter. He might as well be on West Lawn the little good she was doing him. "You're serious?" asked Brennan. He'd said, "Yes, of course."

They had talked of Hardy's escape. "Elopement," he had corrected her. She had told Dromore that she'd let Hardy know the day before that the police were coming to interview him. So he'd be prepared, she explained, so it wouldn't be too much of a shock and set him off. "Or to expiate your own guilt," he corrected her again. He seemed in an up mood, everything considered.

She had never set foot on West Lawn, but she'd toured East Lawn and been called there a few times at night. The buildings, she knew, were identical. Two whole separate buildings for chronics. East Lawn had shocked her. One psychiatrist, hundreds of patients, something over a thousand patients some years back, the women living in gymnasium-size rooms, their beds at one end, their chairs at the other, standing by the window, pacing, staring, some following her and imploring, the floors a polished, shining, creaking hardwood. And the psychiatrist telling her this story, about the Japanese woman who had been there thirty years, working in the laundry, sleeping in her dormitory, and then widening, growing fat, and then losing it quickly and then getting fat again around the middle, and the nurses bringing her to him to be examined. Underneath her dress and tied around her waist he'd found polyethylene bags of saki brewing. Raisins from the tuck shop, rice saved from supper. Marjorie had been around long enough to know it wouldn't have happened quite like that. The nurses would know what was going on and they'd have had their own reasons for bringing the Japanese woman to the doctor. But she'd asked this fat little man with the unlikely name of Bousema what he'd done. "Of course," he'd told her. "We had to take it away." Then he gave her a tour, pointing out a classic case of this and a classic case of that. She had come away angry, but just as angry at the fact of these illnesses as at the way the sufferers were housed and treated. In the middle of the night she had awakened from a dream about East Lawn and startled John with her loud proclamation, "At least the bastard could have let the woman keep her saki."

But Snow didn't lie to her, or his silence was a lie, and then when he'd talked about just going with it, incapable of making a decision for himself, of feeling no reason to choose, no reason to choose to live or die, to leave or go up the hill, how he'd made few right decisions in his life anyway and so why not let Dromore decide his fate, if that's what he wanted to do - when he said this she'd concluded this was bullshit too, but it irritated her enough that she was able to sign the order for transfer without flinching.

So, uncomplaining, not resisting, Robert Snow was transferred to West Lawn. Snow went "up the hill".

"Give him a week," said Dromore to Brennan.

"He wants something," said Brennan. "He's looking for something. He wants to hit bottom."

"We're all looking for something," sighed Dromore, "but West Lawn is hardly the place in which to find it."

Snow let himself be moved, going with the flow, bobbing on the tide like a small piece of cedar bark. What he'd told Brennan was true, at least he felt it to be true, except more and more he was coming to believe the problem was not some fancy philosophical dilemma but a failure of courage, as Karpov had told him. What the hell. Jennifer's letter was clear enough. Nobody from his previous life had found him, called him, visited him, wanted him. Short of killing himself this was as good a choice as any. Self pitying bastard that he was. It'll be an experience he told himself.

He was interviewed by a Dr.Pawlitsky before entering the ward. Pawlitsky sat behind a huge spotless desk. The room was bare, the walls were bare, the color a sort of bilious green, a black telephone, one small shelf containing a few books, the most prominent of which was a very large Bible. Pawlitsky's office had no window. An orderly brought Snow in, left him standing before the desk and took his own place on a chair by the door. Dr. Pawlitsky sat behind his desk, leaning back in a chair, watching Snow, a small smile on his face.

Pawlitsky was short, muscular and bald and had the look of a man who derived satisfaction from the denial of pleasure. He had intense, vigilant eyes, thin tight lips and small hands. Snow immediately saw him as an embalmer, a mortician.

"Well," said Pawlitsky, "I'm honored. We don't usually get physicians here, even unlicensed physicians. They usually go to the private hospitals. No matter. I will tell you though, Robert, that I'm opposed to any kind of special treatment. It doesn't do the patient any good to have special treatment. Here you're Mr. Robert Snow, a patient like any other. Wouldn't you agree, Mr. Snow?"

Snow didn't answer.

"I'm sure," said Pawlitsky, "we'll have some time later for a conversation. Right now I'm just getting acquainted with you. There are a few small rules here in West Lawn and you, like the others, will be expected to obey them. Television is restricted to the hours between four and eight P.M.; a nurse will select the programs; visitors should apply one week in advance of their proposed visit. You understand these last two rules of course. Some television is unsuitable for mental patients and an unanticipated visit by a relative can set a patient back several months." He leaned forward in his chair. "All outgoing mail is screened in my office. We can't have our paranoids pestering the prime minister now, can we? You must bathe once a week, and remain clean-shaven at all times. Shaving materials will be supplied to you each morning and confiscated when you have finished. The hospital food is unfortunately low in fibre and you may find yourself bound up from time to time. If that is the case, please do not hesitate to request an enema. Do you have any questions?"

"I don't think so," said Snow.

"Good. One other thing. Each new patient is examined for venereal disease and lice. You can understand this precaution. Please accompany Mr. Boswick to the examining room. I will join you in a moment."

Snow suffered in silence the indignity of a complete examination. With a wry smile he received the news from Pawlitsky that his prostate was in "fine order". He dressed and followed Boswick up one flight of stairs to the second floor. They passed several unlabelled doors until Boswick selected one that appeared to Snow identical to the rest, and ordinary, perhaps that of a broom closet. The attendant took a key from a large chain at his belt and twisted it in the lock. The door opened and Snow was ushered into a cavernous room, bright from sunlight streaming in through oversize latticed windows. An aide sat just inside the door, back to the wall, reading a magazine. He glanced up at Snow and went back to his reading. Boswick closed the door behind them and led Snow across the hardwood floor. When Snow heard the lock click behind him, he felt a shard of anxiety in his chest. Up until this point he never doubted he could leave Essondale, should he want to. Because he hadn't wanted to leave he felt no great anxiety over the slow erosion of his freedom. With the click of the lock he imagined himself on hands and knees trying desperately to prove his sanity - thus disproving it in the process.

But these thoughts were quickly distracted by the scene before him. He had seen chronic wards before, as a physician, but realized now that he had never really seen them.

On the far side of the room, lined up in tidy rows, were about forty beds, each separated from its neighbour by a foot or so. About twenty men, some sitting, some standing, were scattered around the remainder of the room. It was mid-morning and the ward was already uncomfortably hot. Snow could hear voices but the men were not talking to one another. Yet the mutterings of conversation persisted. He looked around, trying to pinpoint the source of the sound, ready to believe he was hallucinating, and noticed several of the men moving their mouths, talking, - talking to the air, to the floor, and to the wall.

Boswick pointed to the beds. "You'll find an empty one in the last row," he said. "Half the men are working on the ground crew. They come in for lunch at 11:30, till then you're on your own." He turned and walked away from Snow, stopping for a moment to exchange a word with the aide guarding the door. Snow watched him select a key, unlock the door and leave. The orderly went back to his magazine.

"Whacha doin', Bobby?"

Snow looked around to find a big misshapen man shuffling towards him. His body slanted to the left, and his head sat on his shoulders the way a football rests in sand. He came still closer, not stopping until his nose was inches from Snow's and the smell of his breath made Snow gag. Despite the awful odor of the man's carious teeth, Snow held his ground.

"Whacha doin', Bobby?"

"I don't know," said Snow, taking a step backwards.   "I just got here." The sloping man seemed satisfied with that answer and returned to his place three feet from the window.

Not one of the men was doing anything, not engaging in any activity, and yet none was sitting or lying on a bed. Snow surmised that the bed area was out of bounds during the day. He looked for a place to sit or lean and noticed that his fellow inmates were distributed evenly about the room, as if some mighty hand had placed them as pieces in a board game. One man was standing roughly in the centre of the day area, the trunk of his body rocking in and out as if suspended by the top of his head, feet cemented to the floor, rhythmically thrusting his pelvis forward and backward, dipping slightly at the knees. The movement reminded Snow of barroom dancers.

Five men stood by the windows, the slope-sided man with the bad teeth, a tall emaciated, cancerous older man with deep black eyes and three others. The second man was so gaunt that Snow could see the outline of his skull, the hollow under his maxilla normally filled out with flesh. They seemed to be looking at the window rather than through it. Snow noted the view, quite remarkable at first glance. Directly below were the spacious grounds of Essondale, the north side and roof of the admitting wing, and then a lush sweep of farmland, the mighty Fraser River and its Valley, rich and fertile. He experienced a peculiar detachment from the view as one feels the detachment of a superrealist landscape. Behind glass. As if the landscape were preserved - frozen in glass.

One man paced in a four foot area of the floor, walking the perimeter of his square, never varying his step. Another sat and crossed his legs, uncrossed them, crossed them the other way, re-crossed them, his heels and toes rocking on the floor.

While their lives had stopped their bodies carried on living, moving, twitching, decaying, dying. Snow knew he was finally there. He was finally in the madhouse, like Van Gogh, Pound and Munch. If only he could also achieve insanity. But his mind insisted on keeping its journey to the rim of sanity, the outer soft edge of madness, the borderland of numbness and inconsequence.

In his pocket he could feel the envelope with the letter he received the day before he was sent to West Lawn. It was thin, one small page. He knew the words and understood the message: Snow, you are driving me crazy. You want me, when you have me you push me away. I go away only to find you wanting me again. And on it goes. I feel like a ping-pong ball. I know you never really push me away totally - you don't really want me out of your life, but I can't take it any more. I have to get on with my life. I will get over you and you will get over me. Jen. P.S. I'm sorry you are where you are but it's what you really wanted.

So now he was here, at the bottom, finally. There was nowhere else to go, no deeper hiding place. His depression was physical, his fear and his loneliness raged like a fever. He was one of the inmates of West Lawn, a hot body-smelling, cabbage-smelling, floor-creaking place where the bodies of twenty anonymous men twisted in a slow and secret choreography.

TWENTY-THREE

At 11:30 that morning the door opened and let in fifteen additional chronics, back from their cutting, raking, broom sweeping, and picking the grounds of Essondale. These men walked a little straighter than the twenty on the ward, their eyes were slightly brighter. Off the main room of the day area was another room set up with tables, chairs, and a counter. The men walked directly there and the others in the dayroom followed. As they passed along the counter, the orderly and two aides handed each man a plate containing cabbage, mashed potato, and some kind of sliced meat in gravy. At the far end of the counter was a plastic container of spoons. Snow was last through the line and, like the four before him, found the container empty.

Snow took his plate and sat at one of the tables. Each of the other four with no spoons waited until someone finished and then quickly snatched the spoon and began to eat. Snow didn't think he could do it.

"You're new here," said the man opposite Snow, a large man with thick dark hair, a left eye that stared blindly off centre, gravy running down his chin. "Tell me your birthday and your age and I'll tell you the day you were born."

"What?"

"Two dollars says I can tell you the day you were born from knowing your birthday and your age. You know, the day of the week."

"Oh."

"So tell me. Tell me your age and birthday."

"Forty-seven, March 6," said Snow.

"Wednesday," said the madman. "Am I right?"

"I don't know," said Snow. "I don't know what day of the week I was born."

"Pay up. Pay up," said the madman. He took a small, grubby, finely printed book of dates from his shirt pocket and shoved it at Snow. Snow took the book and, while he was trying to find the correct page and line, asked, "Why are you here?"

The madman laughed, swallowed a mouthful of potato, and said, "I killed my stockbroker."

"You what?"

"I killed my stockbroker. Pushed him out a window. Fly away. Fly away Peter, come back Peter. Come back Paul."

"When did you do this?" asked Snow.

"Yesterday. Yesterday morning. The Dow Jones was 941 and the TSE was 1309 and my broker took a fall." His good eye turned cold. "Pay up," he said. "You must pay up."

Snow had been allowed to keep five dollars in his pocket. He dug out two ones and paid the madman.

Several used spoons were available now but Snow had no appetite. The madman saw his reluctance, quickly emptied Snow's food onto his own plate, and devoured it. In the middle of eating Snow's food the madman leaned forward and whispered, "He was wearing panties."

"Who?"

"My broker." Snow ignored this, but the man, finishing the last mouthful of Snow's food, said, "I've got them hidden."

They were all moving now, carrying their empty plates back to the counter. The ground sweepers filed off the ward, the orderly took his chair at the door, and Snow selected a place to sit against the wall and wait for the day to end.

That night, lying in his bed next to thirty-five men lying in their beds, each breathing, snoring, turning, Snow wondered how many days it would take in this place to reduce his mind to a state of perpetual stupefaction. Not insanity, not madness, but stupefaction. Insanity would come, not as release, not as gift, but as a flat blunted torpor. A touch of paranoia would be welcome, a little mania a blessing, even a homicidal impulse might offer relief. He had reread Jennifer's letter looking for hope, but he also knew if he were to find the courage to pull himself out of this hole he must do it without the promise of a golden tit at the end of the struggle. He was alone. And he'd worked hard to make it that way.

TWENTY-FOUR

Matthew Hardy walked the streets of downtown Vancouver feeling exposed without his Stetson. Sometimes he hesitated in the middle of a crosswalk and threw his shoulders back, daring the forces of paranoia to attack him. His feet took him to the familiar territory of Granville Street, where the neighborhood deteriorates perceptibly before spewing onto the bridge crossing False Creek. A small enclave of pimps, hookers, druggies, and winos. Hardy felt safer here. He had ripped the sleeves off Snow's shirt to expose the red scar on his upper arm, his self-inflicted badge of courage. Faces moved by him. The sun was high and warm, the air thick like the air of a barn in April. Hardy's eyes sparkled, his body tensed and coiled, his mind raced.

A confusing mix of fear and fearlessness pervaded his mind. The cops were looking for him; he needed to find his people first, his gang, or get a car, find a room, some food. The farther he walked, the more his appetite dominated his thoughts. He hadn't eaten since the day before yesterday. His first night out had been spent on a bench in Memorial Park sharing a brown-bagged bottle with an old wino. Hardy smelled, his clothes smelled. He was dirty and small, and tall, horny, and hungry all at the same time. He was looking for a fight or a lay and for brief moments he was looking for someone, anyone he knew.

He stepped into the lobby of the Granville Hotel, into the smell of floor oil and old socks.

"Got two bucks?" he asked a white-haired man slumped on a chair in a shabby overcoat.

The old man looked up.

"You got two bucks?" he asked again.

The old man got up from his chair and laboriously climbed the wooden stairs to the second floor. Hardy followed. In his small hotel room of rancid odor and dust- filled air, the old man wrestled two crumpled dollar bills from his pocket and showed them to Hardy. Without taking off his overcoat, the old man undid his belt with arthritic fingers unsteady from wine, and let his pants drop to the floor. Then he pulled his long gray underpants down and sat back on the bed.

Hardy did what he was expected to do, what he had to do, revulsion filtering through a sense of mad pride and sex. The old man held the boy's head almost gently, his fingers entwined in Hardy's dirty blond hair.

When he was spent the old man sobbed and fell forward, pulling Hardy's head to his chest. There were tears running from his rheumy eyes down his sagging cheeks. Hardy let himself be held for a second, then he pushed the old man away, got up, and washed out his mouth in the sink. Hardy looked back, saw the old man still sitting there, his pants on the floor, tears running down his cheeks.

"Hey, old man."

The old man blindly groped for a rag to wipe his face.

"Hey, old man," said Hardy, for a moment touched by the old wino, and for just a moment feeling his own sad loneliness.

"G'wan," said the old man. "G'wan, g't outa here."

When Hardy closed the door behind him the old man was still sitting on the bed, eyes wet, pants draped around his shoes.

In the lobby a queer made a pass at Hardy, a limp-wristed pretty boy. "Fucking queers," said Hardy as he strode out of the hotel, the heels of his tooled leather boots striking hard on the pavement.

Two doors up Granville, Hardy found a hamburger joint, entered it, ordered a cheeseburger, fries, and a milkshake, and sat down in the far corner facing the door. There were only two other people in the restaurant besides the waitress and a cook. Neither appeared threatening in any way. Hardy watched the street through the open door.

Across the street, lounging in a hotel doorway was a young boy -- a spy, someone sent to watch Hardy. The boy looked up and down the street, then strolled out of Hardy's vision, to report in, to tell his superiors where Hardy was. Two blue cars passed, then a bus and then another blue car. Hardy knew there were police in those cars, and they were circling the block. He struggled to understand the significance of blue and the number three. Three is a signal of some kind.

One of the customers finished and left the restaurant. An undercover agent, thought Hardy. He stretched his legs, put his feet on the bench seat opposite, purposely striking a vulnerable, casual pose. Hardy longed for the open air, the prairies, big sky and flat grassland, a world with no walls and no place for danger to lurk unseen. But he forced himself to remain in the restaurant and confront the walls, the furniture, the door.

A customer entered and took a stool at the counter. Hardy felt his heart leap to his throat, his mind race, but he controlled himself. The waitress brought him the cheeseburger, fries, and shake. For a moment he forgot about the conspiracy, the danger, as he ate ravenously, quickly. She returned and left a bill for $3.80. Hardy wished for his Stetson. He took the bill and strolled to the counter. $3.80. He knew he didn't have enough money. The bastards had tricked him. They knew he was only good for $2.00. Time to face them head on. Time to let them know who they were dealing with.

He stopped at the counter and glared at the waitress. She looked up at him, and then looked away. Hardy noticed this and, despite his fear and his madness, despite his anger and his paranoia, he felt sorry for her. She was frightened, small, weak, confused. He didn't want to hurt her. "I've only got two dollars," he said, his voice almost apologetic.

"Pardon me?"

"I've only got two dollars." He said it louder. The cook turned around to look. The customer at the counter studied his coffee cup.

"You owe me three-eighty," said the waitress, checking the bill for confirmation.

Hardy shrugged. "All's I got is two." Suddenly his confidence returned. "He can make up the difference," he said, gesturing towards the man sitting at the counter.

"Now wait a minute," said the cook, coming over to the counter. "Either you got the money or you ain't."

"I ain't got it," said Hardy.

"Well, then you got a problem."

"I got no problem."

"Man, you got a problem."

"Fuck I do."

"When I call the police they'll say you got a problem."

"Stay away from that phone."

The cook stopped short but he suddenly reached underneath the counter and pulled out a handgun. He waved it in Hardy's face. "I bin stiffed too often by punks like you. Siddown over there while I call the police."

The gun was magic to Hardy's eyes, steel and power, fear and power. He leapt over the counter in one swift movement and wrestled the cook to the floor. The waitress screamed and backed away. The customer at the counter ran for the door. The remaining customer, a small elegant Pakistani, sat rigidly in his booth, scarcely breathing. Suddenly Hardy had the gun in his hand; the cook lay on the floor holding his head. The gun felt cold and heavy, it weighed Hardy's hand down and begged to be fired. Images of Seagal, Stallone, and Eastwood flashed through his head. "Don't be frightened now," he said to the girl. She screamed louder. The cook moaned, then, remembering something from another reality, said, "The burger, the meat, it'll burn, gotta turn it."

"Shut up," said Hardy.

He tried the gun in his left hand and then shifted it back to his right, cocking and uncocking it. Dancing behind the counter.

"What do we do now?" said the waitress.

Hardy paused for a moment, thinking. "We wait," he said. They always said that. "We wait." He turned to the grill and flipped the meat patty himself.

Afternoon sun beat down on the pavement outside the door, sending heat waves spiralling upwards. Pedestrians walked past the window. Cars and buses streamed by, coming off the bridge on the way to downtown Vancouver. It didn't take long. A police car pulled up to the curb outside the restaurant and two officers got out to investigate.

TWENTY-FIVE

Snow woke to the noise of thirty-five other men waking. The morning sun streamed in the large windows unhindered by curtains. The air was close and thick with second-hand vapors. The men were being urged out of bed in groups of six or seven and herded to the communal washroom. Once there, they shared three electric razors, passing them down the line.

Snow left his bed and, like the others before him, shed his pyjamas upon entering the washroom. He stood before a sink in a line with six others waiting his turn with the razor. Not until he got it, plugged it in, and applied it to his chin did he realize there were no mirrors above the sink. No mirrors. It struck him as a significant omission. Some of the men in here had not seen themselves for years. Their only reflections came from the eyes of their keepers.

He shaved with the dull and sticky Ronson that pulled his whiskers as much as cut them, standing naked with the others, watched by Boswick and the orderly. When they had finished shaving, Snow and the others padded towards a large shower stall behind a tiled wall. Boswick handed them some pieces of soap. Snow looked for taps and plumbing but found none. Still, the floor was wet, the air humid, water ran down a drain. Then he was hit with a stream of tepid water as Boswick appeared around the corner with a large nozzled hose in his hands.

"Use the soap!" Boswick shouted above the splash of water and the noise of the dancing, squirming, moaning bodies. All seven men were hosed down, their bodies bumping together unconcernedly, shoulders rubbing. They were an ugly lot, a squirming lot, a subhuman group, exposed, wet, cowering, drooling, pissing, huddled together, protecting their genitals from the direct stream, shoving their flaccid wrinkled buttocks at the water. The shower ended as abruptly as it had begun and Snow followed the men into the next room where he was given a damp ragged towel by the orderly.

When he had finished towelling, Snow was handed gray dungarees and a gray work shirt. The night before, according to instructions, he had deposited his shoes in a shoe pile in the far corner of the dayroom. Now he went looking for them and found only six pairs left, none of them his. In fact, four of the twelve shoes remaining in the pile didn't match. At least all were large sizes. He selected two shoes and eased them onto his stockingless feet. No laces.

He was astonished as he watched himself go through all this. Oddly, the absurd deprivation, the dehumanising rituals, the necessity of moving along, of conforming, the total absence of dignity provided a relief from his inner turmoil.

At breakfast call, he moved quickly, determined to get a clean spoon for himself this time. And this morning, despite the food, his situation, and his table companions, he was hungry. After breakfast the workers filed out and Snow, with the remaining twenty men, took his place along the wall of the dayroom, choosing a warming, comforting stream of sunlight in which to sit.

He sat for a long time alone, without stimulation, and for the first hour his mind cart wheeled through highs and lows, pain and pleasure, disappointment, irritation, rage, resignation. He thought of the past and the near past. He wondered what crazy, noxious decisions had led him to this. How did he manage to do this to himself? A butterfly flaps its wings in China. Financial, professional, emotional chaos. He wondered what had become of Hardy and hoped for a visit from Marjorie Brennan. He thought of his daughter. He had a world out there. He had connections. He didn't have the heart to reach for it. He thought of the day fifteen years ago when he had left his family, his daughter's arms wrapped around his legs, crying for a cat that had died one month before. He prayed that the hurt he had inflicted on her would not last. His actions had always cost somebody something. Was there not a way of living that at least had no worse than a neutral effect on the lives around him?

And Jennifer. He had come to believe he couldn't live without her. A strange belief for anyone to have. And yet real. Biological, probably. Some kind of projection of everything that kept the light on, of everything that made it possible to live while disease and death waited patiently. Ah, Jen. For Christ's sake. Before he had met her he had been getting by, maybe shut down, shut down just enough to cope, drinking or not. And then he latched on to her and opened up and the horrors of his rat brain poured out. At forty fucking seven. An adolescent disease, love. And then, not deserving this wonderful new thing, this new life, this new pleasure, happiness, and that most frightening emotion of all, joy, he had sullied it and walked away. Snow, the destroyer.

Sitting against the wall of Ward 2B in West Lawn, the sun on his chest, Robert Snow began to cry. It was the first time since childhood that he had cried in daylight among strangers.

At 11 o'clock that morning the ward door opened and Karpov was wheeled in. Snow saw him but didn't move. He felt both a lifting of his spirit and a wrenching from his reveries to the reality of the dayroom. Karpov pushed himself a few feet into the room and surveyed his new home. Snow sat motionless with the others, waiting. For a moment, just a moment, Karpov's face looked old, tired, and frightened. He sat abandoned in his chair, glancing back as the door locked behind him. Then he saw Snow and his face changed. His shoulders pulled back and he propelled his chair forward.

Snow sat against the wall with his knees pulled up, at first ignoring Karpov. The Bulgarian looked uncomfortable, having for once run out of words. Snow watched him in the silence, saw Karpov's face pleading for recognition, and felt an overwhelming sense of shared sorrow.

"How are you, Victor?" he asked, using Karpov's Christian name for the first time.

"Good, good," said Karpov, brightening now, worry vanishing from his face. "Fine. It only hurts when I breathe. I am bound like a mummy. I have two broken ribs, Robert. That fool nurse thought I was dead. She jumped up and down on me like a peasant flailing his donkey. It is merely one more insult to my body. But how are you my friend? Have you finally found your own purgatory? Are you happy now? Do you have many intelligent conversations with our fellow travellers?"

"They don't talk much," said Snow.

"No? Perhaps I can help them. Perhaps I can bring them enlightenment. But you are happy now, eh? You are happy to be locked away with the fools and murderers."

Snow didn't answer for a moment. Then he said, "I was pleased to see you come through that door."

"You did not look so pleased, Robert. When I saw you there I said to myself, ah, Karpov, there is Robert, sleeping the sleep of the damned. He needs nothing now. He has achieved a null state. He has finally banished his fears, his desires, and even his hatred. He exists solely as a receptor for the sunbeam, absorbing it like a piece of furniture."

"Not quite, Victor. I was thinking."

"And feeling?"

"And feeling."

"Ah, then we are getting somewhere. I, Karpov, the doctor of doctors, will begin the final cure. Tonight Roberto, we will fly away from this place. We will begin the process of repairing your soul."

"You're delusional, Karpov."

"That is true, Robert. But have you noticed one thing about delusions? Life and truth are often trivial. Delusions never are. That man over there," Karpov nodded in the direction of the rocking man, the patient rolling on the balls of his feet, thrusting his pelvis forward and back. "He has the same delusion Hemingway had."

"How do you know?"

"I have ways of knowing these things." He winked at Snow. "And that one over there - he thinks he is Jesus Christ. And that man next to him believes he caused the Titanic sinking. What do you believe, Robert?"

"I'm happy you're here, Victor."

Snow pulled himself up from the wall and took his position at the handles of the wheelchair. "How do you think Hardy's doing?" he asked.

"I've heard nothing," said Karpov. "I don't think he's been brought back yet. But there was an item in the newspaper. Sought for questioning in connection with a death at Essondale. They're looking for him." He took tobacco from his pouch and a paper from his breast pocket and quickly rolled a cigarette in his practiced fingers. "Damn," he said, remembering. "They let you keep tobacco and papers in this place but no matches."

"The orderly may light it for you."

"Then wheel me over there," said Karpov, and Snow found himself quite pleased to be doing something useful for his friend.

TWENTY-SIX

Hardy was mesmerized by the sizzling meat patty, turning it, flipping it, listening to it, the spatula in his right hand, the gun in his left. The waitress had slipped away to the booth in the far corner. The cook lay at his feet, his hands covering his head. Hardy spun around quickly at the words coming from the doorway. "Hold it right there."

A cop in the doorway. Another cop outside. The gun in his wrong hand. The hot hamburger and spatula fell onto the cook. The cook rolled into the back of Hardy's twisting legs. Hardy grabbed at the counter as he fell. The gun in his left hand fired and its discharge flung him backwards on to the cook. The plate glass window shattered and fell across the tables. The room exploded with gunshots, loud, shattering, deadly in Hardy's ears.

Lying on top of the cook, Hardy's mind was clear. All the confusion he had felt over the past few days had been purged by the confrontation he had waited for. He pulled himself off the cook and crawled the length of the counter. He looked around the end. The cops had retreated, to call for backup, he guessed. He shifted the gun to his right hand and sprinted to the back of the cafe.

A small door marked Washrooms opened onto a dingy little corridor with a MENS and a WOMENS, an ashcan, cases of empties, then a back door with a crash bar. He slammed the door open and stumbled into the alley behind Granville Street. He caught his breath in the shadows and then emerged into the bright afternoon sun. He glanced up and down the alley, past the trashcans, rotting produce, poles and telephone wires. Then, sticking to the shadows on the west side of the alley, loped south in the direction of the Granville Bridge. The gun in his right hand took on weight. It felt hot and big and heavy. Ditch the gun. That's what they always did. Ditch the gun. Without changing pace he let it slip from his fingers and fall to the ground.

He had the power now. His stride was long, his body light with the rush of speed in his veins. If only he had his Stetson to protect him. If only the buildings weren't here. If only he were home where he could reach up and touch the sky.

He could hear sirens in the distance and his boots, not made for running, chafed at his sockless ankles. He could smell danger in the air, sense things lurking in the shadows. He ran for the open space he could see at the far end of the alley. A monster loomed up behind a trashcan, rising slowly, a dirty plaid shirt hanging loosely from its shoulders, a brown paper bag tilted to its lips. Hardy sprinted past the drunk, past green doors and orange doors, old fences, barred back windows and broken bottles.

When he came to the first cross street he pressed himself into the shadows against the wall. Cars moved slowly in one direction, all west. Pedestrians crowded the sidewalk. Hardy couldn't see them clearly. Sweat stung his eyes and blurred his vision. He wiped his brow, pushed his hair back. Enemies everywhere. An army searching for him. Not one face recognizable. They would all laugh when he took it in the belly, when he sprawled in the center of the street, blood streaming from his chest, now up on his knees, a trickle of red down his chin, dripping, staining the pavement. The sirens were closer now, a block away. But he had the power. He could leap over the entire street to the alley beyond. He looked west around the corner of a small jewelry shop. Two young girls were looking in the window, one with straw-colored hair and freckles - his sister? Couldn't be. A clone or a dummy sent to distract him. He looked past the girls to the end of the block where the street ran into Granville just at the entrance to the bridge.

He crossed the sidewalk, slipped between two parked cars and stepped into the road. With his eyes fixed on the alley beyond he walked boldly through the traffic, pausing only briefly in the center to raise his middle finger at a driver who was protesting with his horn. Then he was on the other side, in another alley, running south, away from the traffic. He came to another cross street, this one leading under the Granville Bridge on his right, with only a few cars, no pedestrians, dilapidated buildings. The alley beyond dwindled into a gravel path and fell sharply off to the basin below.

Leaving the noise of traffic behind, Hardy picked his way down the gravel slope to the foot of a massive concrete pylon, under the bridge, under the heavy damp concrete, under the rumbling traffic. There he rested for a moment, sitting at the base of the pylon. He began to shrink in size, first a little and then rapidly, until he felt less than five feet tall. Straight ahead were the ruins of sawmills, construction, railroad tracks, and then the thick salt water of False Creek, and beyond that the island of markets, cement works and breweries. Westward, to his right, the embankment curved out and around, under a second large bridge, and then met the open waters of English Bay. Hardy turned in that direction and walked, keeping to shadows, rocks and bushes, heading for the open Pacific.

He paused again under the ramparts of the second bridge. He could feel the rumbling traffic above like a panicked herd on the move. Smells of dead fish, rotting seaweed, urine, and diesel fuel mingled pungently with wispy salt breezes from the inlet. Past the darkness on the other side of the ramps, their masts gently rocking, were several fishing boats and pleasure craft tied to the wharf of a small marina.

Hardy forced himself to think. He was being pursued, the object of a massive dragnet, probably the greatest manhunt in the history of Vancouver. Everyone was suspect. And for what? Jeanie? He hadn't done nothing 'cept take her in the bushes and dog her a little. And then the cops shooting at him. He urged his body to grow and it stretched an inch, then two, but the dark underside of the Burrard Street Bridge held him down. His body craved some open spaces where he could twist and turn and fling his arms, where he could piss without looking over his shoulder, where he could grow back to his full six feet two inches, where he could breathe again.

Hardy scrambled along the steep gravel embankment between the pylons. The noise he made was engulfed in the roar of traffic above. When he reached the far side of the bridge the warmth of the sun cheered him, and, without hesitation, he sprinted down a grassy slope to the marina. He knew nothing of boats or water but an image of himself alone, standing in a dory, defying the raging sea around him, spurred him on. He came to the back of a small bait shop and slipped onto the wharf undetected. He was maybe six-five now, and growing.

The boats with inboard motors were impressive but mysterious. Too many places for ticking bombs.

A twelve- or fourteen-footer with a twenty-horsepower Evinrude seemed to fit his image best. Climbing in now, foot down, boots caught in the planking, the boat twisting, shifting, dipping and lurching under his weight. The motor, like a motorcycle, no, more like a lawnmower. A starter cord, a pull cord. Start, you cunt. Pull. Gas. Open the gas line. Where the fuck's the gas line? Here. Twist it. Twist it. Now it should start. Turn the throttle. What's wrong? Untie the fucking boat. Where is it? There. The knot. Jesus. Fucking knot. Got it. God damn it. Ripped my fingers. Blood. Shit. Red blood. Push away from the dock, drifting now, feeling the ocean underneath, drops of blood falling, spreading on the oily puddle around my boots. The cord, try the cord. Stand up, one good pull. One good pull deserves another.

When the motor caught, Hardy twisted the black handle and felt a surge of power as the stern dug in. The boat spun clockwise, back toward the wharf, then around in a circle, sending a small wave at the marina's proprietor who was running from the bait shop, arms flailing, shouting at Hardy. The cowboy pushed the handle left and right, zigzagging the boat, understanding its steering now, feeling the motor's vibration up through his arm and into his heart.

He pointed the bow toward open water, held the column dead center, twisted the accelerator, and headed out to sea. He settled back as the water spread and grew around him, beneath the sky's shattered reflection. Space, air, freedom like the prairies, and the ominous, powerful, alluring ocean, heaving and sighing beneath him as if it were breathing. A mile ahead small sailboats raced between the buoys off a long sandy beach. On his right over a growing expanse of water the hotels and highrises of the West End leered over English Bay.

Hardy steered a course parallel to the shore several hundred yards away from the bathers, and a mile from the cluster of sails. He knew if he stood now that he would be seven feet tall and the threat of sinking, boots first, beneath the softly rolling sea was tempered by his assurance that he could reach up, grab hold of a cloud, and float across the bay. He felt a surge of sexual energy run through his body. His cock pressed mightily against his pants, urging him on, swelling, ready to plunge itself up an inlet, to the center of the ocean.

Hardy shifted his weight, traded his right hand for his left on the Evinrude, and unzipped his fly. For a moment a circuit was formed between the Evinrude and Hardy's genitals. The propeller spun, the motor vibrated and roared, a great wake curled and bubbled and Hardy, flying now across the waters of English Bay toward Stanley Park and the great maw of the Lions Gate Bridge, shot his wad in heaven's eye.

Afterwards, as he stuffed his cock back into his pants, his eight-foot frame shrank back to six-five and he became conscious of binoculars on the beach. Sun glinting on the windows of the highrises seemed like so many winking eyes. Or sunlight on the steel of a rifle. Crowds of people, bathers, disciples gathered on the sand. Hardy pulled away from them, heading northwest, following the curve of the shoreline, out toward the whitecapped openness of Burrard Inlet.

The swell was heavier here, seeming to roll straight in from the Pacific. Gulls awrked and swooped around a garbage barge being pulled between the dozen freighters anchored in deep water, waiting their turn to brave the First Narrows to get to the sheltered dockyards of Vancouver's Inner Harbour.

The beaches on Hardy's right ended in craggy cliffs rising up out of the water to tree-covered points, massive red cedars and Douglas firs. Rising out of this primeval forest, reaching out like a living thing, forming a graceful arc spanning the waters between Stanley Park and the North shore, loomed the great suspension bridge called Lions Gate.

Confronted by the bridge ahead, flanks of freighters nearby, cliffs on his right, mountains on the north shore, Hardy in his small dory grew small. He revved the motor and headed across the open water to the north shore, crossing a few hundred yards to the west of the bridge. The ocean quickened in response to his Evinrude. Small spitting whitecaps soaked his pants and shirt. The sea under Hardy writhed and turned, racing with the tide under the bridge.

Hardy rode his boat. He dug in his spurs; he pulled himself up in the saddle and shouted into the wind. "Jesus fucking Christ," he screamed, the closest thing to a prayer he knew. The motor sputtered, coughed, and quit, and Hardy's boat was swept broadside with the tide under the bridge high above, twisting and turning in the whirlpools. Hardy stood in his ship now, defying the fates. The boiling sea around him was a herd of cattle, moving, shifting. He shouted at them, "Git. Git along. Move yer ass. Hold it there. Gee- yah. Gee-yah."

The sea grew dark. A cloud slipped in front of the sun. Hardy flung his head back and rode his dory over the hills and across the plain, through the brush and into the storm. A stronger breeze licked at his hair. The boat swept under the bridge and Hardy, his mood being played by the elements like an accordion, began to sing, first in a weak falsetto voice and then, gaining courage, in a deeper, surer baritone. "Onward Christian Soldiers, marching as to war, with the cross of Jesus going on before."

TWENTY-SEVEN

Marjorie was having another bad morning. The day before she had walked, uninvolved, through two admissions, her mind dwelling on conversations with Dromore, on her failure with Snow and Hardy, when she should have been listening to her new patients. She'd have to visit Snow in West Lawn and kick his ass out of there.

The whole week had been bad. The cops had come to talk with Hardy and she'd had to tell them he eloped during the night. They didn't take it too badly, asked if she had any idea where he'd head. She could see them focus now on Hardy. No more questions about other possible suspects. Maybe he did it. No. She could see him doing a lot of things but not that.

She had spent a restless night lying beside but not wanting to touch John, getting up twice to tend to an equally restless Adam. From five on she couldn't get back to sleep. All she needed to do the next day, for her child, for the apartment, at work, the journals she should read, the paper she was promising to write, the patients she should see, ran through her head again and again. She had spent most of the evening vacuuming, tidying, doing wash, making beds. She had the name and phone number of a cleaning lady in her purse she kept forgetting to call. Christ. She had this thing about not wanting some woman her mother's age to clean her apartment. Had to get over it. The light in the hall had annoyed her. John's heavy breathing annoyed her.

About six o'clock John woke with an erection and rubbed it against her thigh.

Marjorie obliged because she felt it might at least help her get an hour's sleep, but she found it difficult to feign pleasure. In the middle she got a cramp in her left calf and had to push John off. He helped to rub her leg, but she could see he was angry and she apologized. She realized he wasn't angry about the cramp so much as her half-hearted lovemaking, but it never did much good to explain that she had trouble getting turned on when she had a lot on her mind, or was angry at him for something. I think, he would say, you might find me more interesting than the goddamn wash. How could she answer that one without starting a fight?

John was up with the alarm at six-thirty and Marjorie, giving up on sleep, reached for a book on the floor beside the bed. She waited until he had left shortly after seven and got up herself, showering, dressing, organizing, rushing as usual, getting Adam up, feeding him, packing his things, wrestling him into the car to drive to the day-care center. In the bathroom she looked long and hard in the mirror, seeing before her a shop-worn woman about forty years of age. So this morning, breaking a vow (again) of several months duration, she applied makeup, tried to hide the darkness under her eyes and the sallow cast of her cheeks. The woman in the bathroom mirror still looked too old and too tired. It wasn't a kind mirror at the best of times. She would look a little better in her Toyota's smudgy rear-view mirror.

After the morning team meeting she was sitting at the nurses' station writing orders on the patients they'd discussed when Dromore came in and sat down beside her.

"Get the news this morning?"

She stopped her writing and looked at him. "No?"

"There was some kind of shoot-out on Granville yesterday. They think your Matthew Hardy was involved."

"Why him?"

"There were people who described him."

Marjorie put the chart she had been working on back in the rack. "So they didn't catch him?"

"Not yet."

"Christ. Where would he get a gun?"

Dromore simply raised his eyebrows.

"He's such a sweet kid when he's well." She was having trouble focusing on the present. Her mind kept going over things she might have said or done, trying to rewrite the recent past. She shivered involuntarily. "I didn't get much sleep last night."

Dromore ignored this. "Are your notes up to date? On Hardy, I mean."

"Yeah. I think they're okay." But she wasn't really sure. How much had she put down on this readmission? And she was probably a couple of days behind. Not only that, but if her notes said something about Hardy being dangerous and she hadn't done anything about it, the shit would hit the fan. Better if she appears to have missed the warnings than to have seen them, recorded them, and not taken any precautions. But what more could she do? Hardy was headed for trouble eventually. And whatever she'd written or not written on the chart would not alter what happened, or was going to happen.

"I think you should check the nurses' notes as well. Make sure they're complete. Make sure there are no surprises in them."

"I wonder where Hardy is now. He must be terrified."

"I know you feel badly about the boy, Marjorie, but the important thing now is to prepare for any investigation that might ensue."

"I understand that."

"Well?"

"It doesn't matter about Hardy. It doesn't matter about Jeanie. All that matters is covering our ass."

"Just protecting ourselves, Marjorie." He got up to leave.

She watched him go. Watched his back, his fat little ass in his three-piece suit. But he was right. She'd have to get hold of herself and go over Hardy's chart before the cops shot him and they called an inquest. She was aware of Melanie watching the two of them from the door.

Melanie said, "Can I talk with you, Dr. Brennan? Alone?"

"Later, Melanie. Maybe this afternoon."

Paul was standing at the rack, also watching her. He said, without looking directly at her, "Would you like a coffee?"

"No, not right now, thanks." She found herself shivering. She leaned against the chart rack and pulled her cardigan around her shoulders.

Paul ignored this. "What do you take in it?"

Marjorie looked at him. "Just cream."

As Marjorie sipped her coffee, holding the cup in both hands, she saw, sitting on top of the filing cabinet, Hardy's brown Stetson. It almost had a life, a personality of its own, now that the cowboy was gone.

After drinking her coffee and dutifully checking Hardy's chart (noting with relief that she had not officially called him an immediate danger or an immediate elopement risk), she walked down the two flights of stairs and out the back door of the admitting wing. There was a hint of autumn in the sky, the breezes slightly fresher, darker clouds gathering in the west, coiling along the Fraser Valley. She walked purposefully up the hill but slowly, as if pushing against a strong headwind. Halfway there the rain started and brought with it the smell of fresh-cut grass. Gulls circled and chattered overhead, driven eastward from the ocean. If she went back for her coat, she'd probably change her mind. Ignoring the rain, Marjorie pulled her sweater tighter around her neck and pushed onward at the same steady pace.

When she reached the entrance to West Lawn she was dripping but refreshed. The large building loomed above her. After a hesitant look at the wire meshed windows, she climbed the three steps and let herself in through the main door. Once inside she sought out the exit sign indicating the staircase. She knew the ward Snow was on; she had filled out the transfer papers herself and she hoped to find it without making enquiries, or explaining her visit to Dr. Pawlitsky. She found the stairs and, holding the iron rail to compensate for a sudden attack of giddiness, climbed to the second floor.

The second floor corridor was empty and windowless. She forced herself to walk the length of the hallway looking at each unmarked door in turn. For a moment she saw herself trapped in this corridor of anonymous doors, searching forever, without the courage to try a single one. Finally, gathering conviction, she chose a particularly worn and battered door and reached for the handle.

At that moment she realized that the door would be locked and, taking a small step back, she knocked. Very quickly it opened from inside and Marjorie stepped through. The aide appeared surprised to see a damp woman standing beside him.

"I'm Dr. Brennan," said Marjorie. "I've come to interview one of your patients. Robert Snow. Oh, I see him there now, thank you."

She walked toward Snow quickly before the aide had a chance to say anything. Snow was sitting by the window talking with Karpov. The fifteen or so other men in the room shifted their postures one by one until all but two were looking at Marjorie.

Snow looked up, Karpov too. They were wearing hospital- issue pants and shirts and she noted with dismay how little Snow's degrees and background protected him from fitting in.

"Where can I talk to you alone?" said Marjorie.

Snow looked at her dripping on the floor. "I think we could use the nurse's office. She's never in."

"Which one is that?" asked Marjorie, beginning to shiver.

"Over there," said Karpov. "The second door." He wheeled his chair over to the aide. "Dr. Brennan would like to use the office," he said, "would you open it for her?"

"You sure she's a doctor?"

"Of course I'm sure."

The aide put down his magazine, walked across the room, and unlocked the office door. Snow followed Brennan inside. He switched on a light and closed the door. Marjorie sat on the edge of the small desk. Snow stood by the door.

"I'm not sure why I came," she said lamely.

"You're wet."

"It started raining on the way up."

Glancing around the office he reached for a small pile of towels. "Here," he said. "Dry yourself off. You're shivering."

Marjorie took a couple of white towels Snow offered her.

"It's just a summer rain," she said. "You can't catch cold from a summer rain." She towelled her hands and her face, then fluffed her hair as Snow watched her. She said, "I thought you would want to know about Hardy."

"What about Hardy?"

"He was in some altercation with the police. Yesterday afternoon. They're still looking for him."

"Yeah, well, Christ. I suppose it's inevitable."

"They're convinced he killed Jeanie."

"Well, there's a guy up here..." He shifted on his feet. She stopped towelling and looked at him. "A patient in here, some kind of idiot savant, says he has a pair of panties hidden. And I remember the rumors about Jeanie's being missing."

"You think they're hers?"

"That's not exactly what he said."

"Christ. I'd have to talk to Pawlitsky. Get him to authorize a search."

"Maybe Victor and I can get him to show us."

"That might be faster. And then let the police know. They could come from anywhere." She shrugged.

Still standing he said, "Why did you come all the way up here?"

She folded her arms. "I wanted to know if you were ready to leave yet. If you'd seen everything there is to see. If you're ready to give up this masochistic...thing of yours."

He sat in the chair. "I've got my name on the list to see
Pawlitsky."

"List?"

"That's how it works up here. You go through the nurse. She puts
you on a list. Maybe you get to see the doctor in a week or two."

"Christ. You're willing to wait that long?"

"I'm learning some things."

"About yourself?"

"About myself."

"I wish I understood you, Snow."

"A few people have said that."

"Dr. Brennan, there's an outside call for you."

Marjorie was sitting in the nurses' station again poring over some
old medical records. She pulled herself from the chair, walked over
to the reception desk, and took the telephone. She expected to hear
John telling her he had to work late, multiple trauma case or
something, or the day-care center saying Adam had a fever, a broken
tooth, or something worse.

"Dr. Brennan here."

"One moment please, I'll connect you," said the hospital operator.
And then Marjorie could hear background traffic noises, breathing,
and a faint, young boy's voice.

"Doc?"

"This is Doctor Brennan."

"Doc. It's me...Hardy...Mat Hardy."

"Where are you?"

The nurse looked up.

"I'm in a phone booth, downtown...I'm in trouble."

"I know. I mean I know you're in trouble."

"I can't talk long. Gotta keep moving."

"Where are you?"

Long pause. Marjorie glanced over at the nurse, who returned to
her work. Marjorie kept looking at her. She got up and left.

"I can't tell you, doc. They're after me. They're gonna kill me.
They got dogs on my trail. Hey, d'you hear that clicking? Get off the
phone, creeps. The line's tapped, Dr. Brennan. Be careful what you
say."

112

"Those are just normal telephone sounds."

"Yeah, well. I'm cold."

"Don't you have any clothes?"

"Only what I was wearing, you know, Snow's shirt."

"Have you had anything to eat?"

"Not since yesterday."

"What happened, Matthew?"

"I dunno. I went for a hamburger is all. I'm having trouble remembering it. The cops were watching me, closing in."

"You had a gun."

"It wasn't mine."

She walked the phone around the desk and sat down. "You shot at the police."

"I...there was a gun, yeah. I had a gun, but I didn't shoot at no one. It all happened pretty fast."

"You should give yourself up to the police, Matthew."

"I can't do that," said Hardy. And Marjorie knew he couldn't. She wondered about her duty in this situation. Should she be holding Hardy on the phone while police traced the call? Should she be trying to get him to reveal his location? Should she be trying to help him?

She asked, "Why did you call me?"

"I need some clothes...and a little money."

"You can't get away from the police, Matthew. They'll find you sooner or later."

"Not where I'm goin'. I'm goin' way up north, logging camp or somethin'. Can you get me some clothes?"

"Maybe."

"Yeah?"

"I need to know where you are."

"You promise no cops or nothin' like that? You come alone?"

Marjorie hesitated. He sounded down now, off his high, no longer psychotic, a frightened child. And he was her patient, after all. "All right." she said.

"Okay then. I'm on Water Street. Hotel Europe or somethin'. The third floor."

"Hotel Europe?"

"Like that, on Water Street."

Marjorie looked out onto the ward.

Hardy said, "When you coming?"

She found herself answering, promising. "Tonight, early evening sometime."

"Okay." The line went dead.

"Matthew?"

Marjorie hung up the phone.

She went back to her charts but found she couldn't concentrate. She knew she should call the address in to the police but she also knew, God help her foolish heart, she was going to go through with the clothes drop. He sounded pathetic, harmless, frightened, lonely. He was first and foremost her patient. And surely some honest kindness on her part could not be entirely wrong. Besides, she had promised. Maybe she could talk him into taking some pills and going to the police with her. It could save his life. And if he wouldn't come in, she could notify the police afterwards. He was still, after all, her patient, she reassured herself again.

Karpov seemed fascinated by the idiot's skill. Sitting in his wheelchair across the table from the big man with the dead left eye, Snow at his side, he kept giving him dates in history and then thumbing through the idiot's little red book to check them. He tried the reverse as well, giving him the third Wednesday in January 1946, and then checking the date the idiot told him in his high staccato voice. He said, in an aside to Snow, he must have a system, and then later, no, he's memorized the whole goddamn book. "Imagine," he said, "Enough room in your head to stick a phone book. All those synapses going to waste. Try this: November 3, 1963." He turned back to Snow. "I know that one without the book."

Snow, who had learned the man's first name, said, "Richard, tell me about your stockbroker again."

Richard's dead left eye pointed over Snow's shoulder. "Not a stockbroker," he said.

"Not a stockbroker?"

"Not a stockbroker."

"You told me about killing your stockbroker."

"You're a murderer."

Karpov, watching this exchange, smiled at Snow and said, "Our savant has other insights."

"Richard," said Snow, "You told me about killing your stockbroker and keeping his panties."

"Her panties," said Richard.

"Okay," said Snow. "Right. Her panties. Can you show them to us?"

"No."

"February 6, 1941," said Karpov.

Over dinner that evening Marjorie said, "I have to go out for a while tonight." She took another mouthful, trying to convey only moderate interest in John's response.

John was saying, "So there we were doing this routine cholecystectomy and Macdonald feels around, seeing what else is in there and suddenly he lets out this loud 'Shit' and pulls his hand out like something bit him. I fucking loved it. He's the guy just loves to mutter through his mask 'Looks a little blue' when I've got all this high-tech telling me the oxygen's fine."

Marjorie repeated herself, "I've gotta go out for a little while."

Looking up now, John said, "Oh?"

"I'm taking some old clothes to a patient. You won't mind, will you? Looking after Adam, I mean. I'll only be gone an hour, an hour and a half."

"Thought that's what you have social workers for."

"This is a special case. An old man, about your size. I'm taking him those things we were giving to Amity."

"The stuff we sorted last Sunday?"

"Uh huh."

"My good brown sweater?"

"It's not good. It's not even brown any more. Adam, finish your peas."

"My mother gave it me for Christmas."

"You never wear it."

"That's true. Where you taking the stuff?"

"It's one of those senior citizen complexes in the West End." She took the spoon from Adam and shovelled some potatoes and peas at his mouth. He spat it out, said, "Ice cream."

"Little more of this first."

"I could drive, if you'd like."

Marjorie looked at him. She couldn't believe her ears. Tonight of all nights he offers. "It's okay. It's not a bad part of town, just take me a few minutes."

Marjorie changed in their bedroom. Skirt, blouse, jacket, a sensible pair of shoes, purse, and she might pass for a social worker, if someone were to ask, except they don't dress this way anymore, maybe a probation officer. She checked herself in the mirror. This was insane. What was she trying to prove? Well, at worst she'd be in and out and then she'd call the police. At best he might not be there. She gathered the bundle, car keys, said goodbye to John and Adam, stealing a spoonful of ice cream on the way, told them, again, unnecessarily, she'd be back very soon.

She drove down Water Street slowly, glancing from side to side trying to make out the names of several small and dirty hotels. It wouldn't be as easy as she imagined. One building offered beds for $10.00 a night, $45.00 weekly, its name unreadable. Used furniture was being sold beneath a Laundromat sign; a variety store had arisen in the ruins of a radio and television outlet. Men and a few women loitered in the doorways. She pressed on, deeper into Water Street, closer to the docks. She was ready to give up, a little relieved, when she saw it: Hotel Europa.

Marjorie found an empty spot on the opposite side of the street and parked her Toyota. She locked it carefully and walked purposefully across the street, the bundle of clothing in her arms, purse over her left shoulder. She remembered somebody's advice - always look like you know where you're going when walking through a neighborhood like this. She hesitated before the entrance, a little short of breath. She stopped to inhale deeply and, as she did, a door twenty yards away opened and three men reeled out onto the sidewalk. Their shadows were long, the tops of their heads back-lit in yellow halos. It would be dark very soon. Marjorie hurried in through the door of Hotel Europa, up two steps to the landing.

116

In the dimly lit foyer of the old hotel a night clerk sat behind a high oak desk, a green shade on his forehead. He was watching a flickering television screen at the end of the counter and he didn't look up until Marjorie spoke.

"I've come to see a client of mine...I'm from the city welfare department. I'm a social worker."

Turning toward her he let his expressionless gaze pass slowly from her waist to the growing blush at her hairline.

"He said he was on the third floor," she added.

"Name?" said the clerk, coughing into a yellowed handkerchief.

Would he be using his own name? "Hardy. Matthew Hardy."

"There's a kid in 304," said the clerk. "Came in with no bags I could see. Blond, tall kid. Signed himself C. Bronson."

"That's probably him. Is he in his room?"

"He ain't come past here."

"Could I go up to see him, deliver these clothes?"

"Up to you lady." And he spat again into the soiled handkerchief.

Without touching the handrail, Marjorie walked up the first flight of stairs. A single light bulb hanging by its wire illuminated the rubber runner on worn wooden stairs. The second flight had no light at all and Marjorie fought the temptation to glance over her shoulder. On the third floor her footsteps echoed loudly. The smell of old frying oil mingled with body odors. Marjorie found 304 and knocked.

Hardy's voice answered. "Who's there?"

"It's me. Dr. Brennan. I've brought you some clothes."

"Just a minute. I'm gonna unlock the door. Don't come in until I say so."

Marjorie heard him at the door and then walking away.

"All right. Come in slow."

Marjorie entered, muttered, "Oh, shit," to herself, and, "Brennan, you must be fucking certifiable." Hardy was sitting on a dresser against the wall opposite the door, watching the door, vigilant, his booted feet dangling above the floor, a strange object in his right hand, something that looked like a sock stuffed with marbles. "Christ, he's high again."

"Quick, shut the door," said Hardy.

Marjorie did as she was told. Her moment to run had passed. She chose the lower of two chairs in the room, thinking to herself, "Don't intimidate, don't provoke. Look defenceless." After sitting down in a slow, deliberate fashion, she said, "I've brought you some clothes."

Hardy moved off the dresser and sat on the edge of the bed facing Marjorie. His eyes sparkled.

"Lessee what you got."

Marjorie pushed the bundle of clothes at him, watched him tear the plastic bag and paw through the gift like an impatient child.

"These look okay. They'll do me. Belong to your old man?"

"My...right, yes."

"Tell him thanks," said Hardy.

"I brought you something else," said Marjorie, her confidence growing. She opened her purse and then, under Hardy's watchful eye, withdrew a bottle of pills. "Chlorpromazine. I'd like you to take some medication."

Hardy slapped his sock into the palm of his left hand. "It ain't much, but it's all I could think of." He slapped it again. "Swiped the sock from a drunk in the alley. Pow. Works pretty good though. Full of pebbles from the beach. Not as good as lead shot or a knife if you know how to use one, but still pretty good. Crack a skull easy." He grinned at Marjorie.

"I really think you should take two of these tablets, Matthew."

Hardy snatched the bottle with a movement so sudden that Marjorie gasped. He put the bottle on a small table beside the bed and then, saying, over and over again, "This is what I think of your goddamn fucking pills," he smashed it with his pebble filled sock. He smashed it again and again as Marjorie, white-knuckled, pushed herself deeper into the chair. The vial shattered, pills scattered. Still he swung hard at the table.

"All right. All right." Her voice was strangled. "No pills. You don't have to. I won't ask again."

Hardy smashed at the scattered white tablets as if they were insects, his face red, his biceps tensed. He smashed at them for the years and months they had held him down, for the days they had turned his blood to porridge, for the hours they had stiffened his muscles and alienated his mind from his body.   He crushed them for all the things they represented, and most of all he crushed them because he knew he needed them. Then his eye caught Dr. Brennan digging her nails into the chair, her face white and struggling for control. He had frightened her. It was in his power to do so. Had she been a man who had dared to enter his room he would have relished and prolonged this moment. But a woman...

"Did I scare you?" he asked, brushing the white crumblings to the floor. "I don't mean to."

He's doing it again, thought Marjorie. A madman, a lunatic, and then suddenly a sensitive young boy, but with fire burning out of control behind his eyes. She had to clear her throat to speak, "Yes. Yes you did."

He watched her now, and Marjorie allowed herself a glance around the room. A single window opened onto an alley fire-escape. Tattered white curtains fluttered against torn wallpaper. It had grown dark outside and the room's two forty-watt light bulbs bathed the scene in sepia tones. She was a fool to have come. His eyes were appraising her and there was more than a hint of sexual awareness in them. His psychotic mind was wondering why she had come. It would soon reach some inevitable conclusions. And Marjorie wasn't absolutely sure those conclusions would be wrong. Had her unconscious let her down? Had some masochistic impulse dragged her here to confront terror, to put her hand in the fire, to be raped, to be brutalized?

Or did she come simply because she believed she could reach him and help him...help the frightened young boy betrayed by his own chemistry? Would the nice answer to her question, the answer her father might have given...would that be going deep enough? Or must she prowl around in the darker recesses of her mind to find out what she's doing here? Or should she stop all this self-analysis horseshit and get the hell out? Better say something, Marge old girl, better get control of the situation.

"What happened, Matthew? After you left the hospital? What kind of trouble are you in?"

Hardy got up from the bed and leaned against the window frame. "Ain't no trouble can't be fixed. I'm getting close now. I can really feel it comin'." He sat down opposite Marjorie and stared deep into her eyes. "Don't laugh when I tell you this, but sometimes I get the feeling I can fly."

"It would be nice to be able to fly, Matthew."

"Yeah, and sometimes I get the feeling I could fuck ten women at once." Marjorie let that one go by.

"Have you had anything to eat? You've got no money."

"No problem. I just go blow some old wino for a couple of bucks."

The image made her feel like gagging. "You should come back to the hospital, Matthew. You can't...survive out here. Not yet anyway."

"Don't you remember, doc? Don't y' know? They're gonna kill me. They set me up for this and now they're gonna kill me." He got up and paced around the room as he talked. "This is what they wanted right from the beginning. A final showdown. I'm ready for 'em. It'll cost 'em to take me out."

"How are you feeling, Matthew? I mean your mood."

He spun towards her. "Strong, fine. And I've got..."

"Got what, Matthew?"

"Doesn't matter."

"Something special?"

"Yeah. Power, man. I've got so much power runnin' through my body."

"From where? Where does it come from?"

Hardy suddenly went shy. "Who knows. Maybe the power station up the street. Maybe..."

"Maybe from God?"

"Yeah. Maybe from God."

You're more in control now, said Marjorie to herself. Just ease him down gently and get out of here. Hardy's face was grimacing like a man trying to hold a grin and afraid of losing it.

"You're frightened as well, aren't you, Matthew?" Before she finished the sentence Marjorie knew her timing was bad.

"Jesus fuck! I'm not scared of nobody, least of all you and your fucking pills and your fucking hospital." His shoulders tensed and his right fist clenched as if to strike but instead he jumped on the bed in his boots, bounced three times, and landed on the other side. She saw that his grimace was holding, his eyes more demonic than ever.

"I think the clothes will fit you," she said. "I have to go now." She moved to the edge of her chair.

"Don't go yet." It was both command and plea. And almost as an afterthought, "You didn't tell the police where I'm at?"

"I didn't talk to the police."

"If you'd had of..."

"They don't know you're here."

His face softened again, suddenly. He reached into his pocket and brought out an awkwardly folded piece of writing paper. "It's a letter to my little sister. Would you send it for me?"

Marjorie took the opportunity to stand up. Keeping a good distance between them, she reached out to take the letter, her mind silently coaching: just give me the letter, stay cool, relax, one more minute, just let me go.

Hardy hesitated, then released the paper and turned his back to Marjorie. It was some kind of test.

She moved to the door, opened it quickly, and casually said goodnight. Glancing back, she saw Hardy standing in the middle of the room watching her, his face now sad and lonely. Or was she just seeing what she wanted to see?

In the corridor Marjorie's knees felt weak, her pulse erratic. She walked down the two flights of stairs unsteadily and very slowly.

Karpov was saying, "Why are you so interested, Robert? In these pink panties?"

Snow was sitting on a wooden chair waiting for an opportunity to search Richard's mattress. "I don't know. Maybe my depression's lifting. Maybe if I don't focus on something I'll go mad in here."

"Maybe you want to live again."

"How do you know they're pink?"

"What?"

"The panties. Jeanie's panties."

"White, pink, what difference? We don't know they're Jeanie's."

Snow looked at him. "You don't think much of women. At least your poetry is pretty angry."

Karpov wheeled away one rotation and back. "Now he rises from the dead he's an analyst. Dr. Snow, first you become God and then you can analyse Victor Karpov."

"Okay. I'm sorry. It's nothing to do with it."

"I will find these troublesome panties for you, Snow." He spun in his chair and rolled toward the sleeping section of the large dormitory.

"I'm back." Marjorie shed her purse and sweater in the hallway. "I said I'm back." Too quickly, defensively.

"I'm in here," came John's voice. "I put Adam to bed." She heard a rustling of newspaper in the living room. Marjorie moved across the entrance, suddenly unsure of herself. She was trying to be natural but by consciously trying she could no longer remember whether she should go first to John or Adam.

"I'll check on Adam," she said.

In the baby's room, as always, the world changed. For a moment her complete attention was focused on the sleeping little boy, his arm curled around a stuffed giraffe, two cars and three trucks scattered on the sheets. How could I want anything else when I've got it all here? She removed the toys, leaving the giraffe in place, pulled his blanket up to his neck, and bent to kiss him. The sweetness of his breath was perfume to her nostrils but she couldn't help noticing the food on Adam's face. She wiped at it with the edge of his blanket. She tiptoed out of the room. She tried to tell herself John's silence could mean that he hadn't noticed the time. She walked into the living room, slipped off her shoes, and sat beside him on the couch.

"Is there any wine left?" she asked.

"A little, I think. In the kitchen." His eyes remained fixed on the paper.

"Would you like some as well?"

"Hnnnnh."

Marjorie got up from the couch and walked to the kitchen in her stockinged feet. He called out after her, "I'm on duty next three nights in a row."

"Why three in a row?" she asked, returning with one glass of wine.

"Just the way the schedule worked out, that's all."

She curled her feet on the couch, leaned into him a little.

"Paper says one of your loonies was in a shootout yesterday."

Marjorie choked on her wine. "My..."

"From the hospital. Escaped mental patient in shootout with police. Front page." John folded the newspaper and laid it in his lap. "They should have tighter security around a place like that."

Marjorie knew he was just trying to get a rise out of her. "Let's not talk about work. Not tonight."

"Was he one of your patients?"

"Yes."

"You didn't tell me about it."

"I just wanted to forget about it. When something like this happens we talk enough at the hospital."

"You must have been quite upset." He softened and smiled at her. Marjorie sensed the change and she knew she could make it work if she let him comfort her now. If she let him do his male protective thing, her unexplained lateness would be forgotten. But she couldn't. She was angry at his sullenness and she couldn't lean into his arms.

"These things happen," she said.

John let out a sigh and laid his head on the back of the couch.

"What's that all about?" said Marjorie. She kicked herself. She could have let it go. But something made her want to make him say what he was thinking.

"Wha'd'ya mean, 'What's that all about'?"

"You know. The sigh and everything."

"I was just trying to help...to understand. That's all." He said it in a hurt voice, a voice that Marjorie found irritating.

"You're angry at me," she said.

"I'm not angry at you, goddamn it. Something's been bothering you for a week or two. I thought maybe if I found what it was and tried to talk with you..."

"It's your tone of voice," said Marjorie.

"What's wrong with my tone of voice?"

"It's...maybe I'm just tired. Maybe I am upset. But sometimes when you...I don't know. I'm sorry I said it. You just sound sometimes like you're putting me down, or you're annoyed with me."

"I don't mean to."

"I know. I know. I'm just having a bad week. Sorry." She leaned into his shoulder. "Forgive me?"

"Yeah, sure, why not? I'll never find what's going on."

They smiled at each other now, a momentary truce, a softening. He could be quite sweet, she thought. "Would you like a glass of wine now?"

"That would be nice."

Marjorie extricated herself from the couch and walked to the kitchen. When she was ten feet away he said, "You took a long time to deliver those clothes tonight."

She continued to the kitchen in order to answer where he couldn't watch her. "You know these old people. They don't get much of a chance to talk to anybody. I didn't realize it was so late." When she returned with the wine their truce held. He seemed to accept her explanation.

That night in bed he stroked her small breasts carefully, as if puzzled and unsure of himself, trying unsuccessfully to make her nipples rise and harden. Marjorie's thoughts were far away. When he stopped and let his hand slide from her body she looked over at the hall-lit profile of his face. She read confusion around his eyes and hurt on his lips. Moving toward him, she ran her hand through the hair on his chest, caressing his nipples. He turned and smiled at her, warily, rolled over, and began to kiss her breasts and her chest, sucking for a minute on nipples that were now responding. His head slipped to her belly and on down but her hands checked him there and brought him back to face her. She spread her legs and helped him enter. She was dry and winced. Pulling himself back, propped on his right elbow, Paul reached over Marjorie for the Vaseline jar. He entered her again and she tried to concentrate on their lovemaking, on his body, on the sensation in her vagina. He called her "Butter..." and came. She pushed against him, just excited enough now to want the release of orgasm, just enough to feel the irritation of an unfulfilled promise. She pulled him deeper as he shrank away, their timing off, as usual. She dropped her hands to her sides, resigned. Christ, I shouldn't have got into it, let myself get worked up. She could ask him... No, she couldn't ask him.

When John rolled on his back she gave him the Kleenex and looked for a moment at his satisfied but still wary face. "Goodnight, Butter," he said.

A few years before she had thought the name was cute, endearing. "Better than Marge," he had said. Anything's better than Marge she had said. "After all," he had said, "You're something of a high-priced spread. I mean the real thing, the genuine article."

"Just another dairy product to dip your prawn in," she had replied, surprising him with the vulgarity.

She was restless now. Her thighs itched for something else, something more. She visited the bathroom, looked in on Adam, and then sat for a long time with a glass of milk at the kitchen table. Her mind drifted back to Matthew Hardy. She was way past the moment she could call the police about him. What the hell was she doing? What was she trying to prove?

When she finally went back to bed her last thought before falling asleep was I should have taken the Stetson to him.

TWENTY-EIGHT

Hardy pulled on a shirt and a brown sweater from Marjorie's bundle, eased himself out the window and climbed down the fire-escape. He dangled briefly from the bottom rung and then dropped easily to the pavement a few feet below. After crouching for a moment in the shadows to get his bearings, he set off for the lights of East Hastings with a certain jauntiness to his walk. Messages were coming to him; his tentacles enveloped the city. It was not clear yet but soon, very soon .... Traffic menaced by on the road; gargoyle faces on misshapen bodies passed him on the sidewalk, gathering to watch and listen, perhaps to learn.

Traffic lights and neon signs danced within the glitter dome of mercury lamps. Poles, wires, trashcans. Hardy looked at the dimly lit storefronts, some with Chinese characters, others with signs in Italian and Portuguese. Outside the first tavern a toothless old man sloppily begged him for 25 cents. Hardy brushed the man aside and entered the port holed swing doors. A paint-peeled and dusty sign above read Ladies and Escorts. He found a table in the corner of the large beverage room and scanned the occupants. Beer glasses and overflowing ashtrays littered the table tops. Nearest to Hardy was a man sitting alone, occasionally speaking to an invisible friend across the table. At other small round tables they sat in threes and fours, talking, laughing, arguing. A few Indians drank on his left, their bodies absorbing the beer like water balloons. A couple of Native women sat with the white men.

Hardy felt the vibrations. He listened to the messages. The hum and buzz of expletives, the cadence of slurred convictions, watery eyes watching one another. A table flared and drunks lurched to their feet, pushing chairs over. Waiters converged, settled the disturbance quickly and put more beer on the table. Hardy listened for instructions. A message from the Redman. A word from the Italian. A plea from the kid in the vomit stained shirt. All he got was a garble of self hate, a need to lash out in the dark. Flail your body, subdue the spirit, rend the putrid flesh. 'Kill yourself' was the message he received, so Hardy left before the waiter found him.

On the street again Hardy headed west. Within two blocks the storefronts changed; the crowd was better dressed. He looked in the windows of small boutiques, antique shops and coffee houses. He listened to the people. They were having fun. They pursued pleasure with the preparation and intensity of warfare. They hovered in the light just above skid row, like children drawn to the edge of a swamp, occasionally stepping over or around a vagabond who had wandered one block too far west. Hardy looked into their faces. He saw them rushing somewhere and he followed. And when they rushed back he followed too. He listened to their anxiety, their desperation. He felt them clawing at one another. They wanted him to excite them; they wanted him to lead them; they wanted Matthew Hardy to set them free. He moved through the crowd feeling their eyes, their pressure. They danced around him like flies on the eye of a cattle beast. They came at him too quickly and mingled with the dreams of his childhood. He saw a man turn into a woman before his eyes, and he saw men who were not men and women who were not women and he felt as if the world and his own mind were rapidly disintegrating.

Chaos reigned and he strove to keep his head a foot above the whirling eddies, faces, light, colours, movement. He saw a man carrying a sword and a woman said to him as she passed, let's you and I fuck. He turned to find her and she was gone but the words left a trail of stardust in his mind. Let's fuck, let's fuck, let's fuck ... the words hummed through the crowd. A man, a queer, a faggot, touched his sleeve and Hardy recoiled. For a moment he pressed against the side of a building, next to the coin filled case of a street musician. And then he slipped around the corner and ran down a side street. He ran a block, stopped, and caught his breath. He turned into an alley to rid himself of the noise and crowd. Darker now, quieter, he turned another corner.

Directly in front of Hardy, lounging against their bikes under a backdoor light, were two men in black leather jackets, their sequins, chains and fancy rings shimmering in the dark. Friends or foes? Hardy did not know. He felt the pebble filled sock in his pocket. He stood still and caressed its lumpiness. The one with the great red beard, a pair of shades, and a gut hanging over his jeans, beckoned to Hardy. Hardy wished for his Stetson with all his might. He walked

slowly forward. Bikers. Back home with his jacket and his horse,
Hardy was a biker as well. These guys were like cowboys off the
range. Hardy watched the two in front of him. He felt their
vibrations: Kill the queer they said. Bugger the faggot the chorus
echoed. All men are brothers said Hardy. The bikers laughed.
Jesuuuus said one, we got ourselves a Hary whatsit. Krishna said the
other.

"Got a smoke?" asked Hardy, being cool and hip, one hand
feeling the pebbles in his pocket.

"You're too young to smoke ain't ya sonny."

"That's right," said Hardy, but his mind was not taking it in.
Smoke, fire. Where there's smoke there's fire, it was saying to him.
His hand took the pebble filled sock out of his pocket, feeling the
weight on his arm. Hardy wasn't aware he had it out and visible until
the fat one said, "Ah, the little boy wants to play does he."

They got up from their bikes and moved towards him. Hardy felt
the danger now and once again it fueled his mania. He could move;
he could dance; he could deek; he could thrust. Did they not realize
the forces he could call upon to support him? He stood his ground in
the shadows of the alley, ready, avenging. He didn't see the third man
behind him until too late. Lake the crack of a whip, the first blow hit
him between his shoulder blades. Hardy pitched forward into the
arms of red beard who, the cowboy noticed, smelled like a sow in
heat. The biker shoved him back; Hardy tripped over the legs of the
second man, and tumbled to the pavement. He swung his sock, wildly
scattering pebbles ineffectually up and down the alley. The first boot
hit him in the side of the chest. Hardy gasped for breath and tried to
release his soaring spirit from its already prone and injured body. He
got to his feet and was knocked down again. He crawled across the
pavement and scrambled behind a garbage can but the punishment
continued. Three men, ten men, a hundred men were attacking him.
Pretty boy, pretty boy they said. They think I'm a queer thought
Hardy. I'm not a queer he gasped. I'm a --- , but he couldn't think of
the word. They laughed and hit him again. Blood trickled from
Hardy's nose and his mouth as he doubled up protecting his stomach.
Protecting his genitals. He knew they were after his genitals. Sheets
of pure colour blinded him. He grabbed for legs and boots. He tried
to stand again. For a moment he saw the faces leering down at him,
three, six, ten, thick red lips oozing a sort of intense sensuality, and

then he fell into the arms of merciful darkness, thinking, they love me
as they loved Christ.

TWENTY-NINE

Look at the slatherings of Black Angus, said the slope-sided man.
Archie danced on to the song in his head. Sunlight caught dust
particles spiralling upwards as each man turned to his own voices.
Karpov smoked a cigarette and looked out the window while Snow
sat at his feet wondering. Are you ready, asked a young man kneeling
at his side. Not yet, not yet, answered Snow. Are you too old, asked a
sightless old man sitting in a chair. Not too old, said Snow.

"You're talking to yourself," said Karpov. "It is an early sign of
degeneration of the imagination."

"Yours or mine?"

"Theirs," said Karpov. "When time loses its pace, its measure,
movement becomes important. Life must have one or the other."

"I understand," said Snow, "that they're really the same thing.
Time and motion, I mean."

"Very true, Robert, very true. The movement that creates our
time of death goes on without us. The universe evolves no matter
what we do or don't do. But the movement that creates our time in life
is up to us."

Karpov paused to suck on the butt of his cigarette, apparently
satisfied with his last pronouncement, while Snow watched his
fellows. Some had tortured faces, sweating, twisted, as if they had just
completed ten-mile runs, working at living or staying alive, their outer
worlds taken from them, their definitions gone. An inner demon was
energizing the computer in its bonds, scanning, organizing, trying to
make sense of what it saw, failing, and showing the agony of failing,
going nowhere. Others seemed to trade the beds, the floorboards and
their misshapen compatriots for a world of their own, drifting away
on inner journeys, not exotic and colorful, but plain, dull, simple and
secure. Their faces reflected a certain degree of comfort. Still others
had simply vacated their minds like citizens of a decaying urban
center. Here a man might learn to live without desires, regrets, or any
strong emotion.

"Push me around the room, Robert. That's better, a little movement. Did you know Hitler's architect walked around the world sixty times within the walls of Spandau?"

"Did it give him life, Victor?"

"I think he achieved a certain state of grace, Robert."

"So, did you find anything?"

"I was waiting for you to ask."

"I'm asking."

"There is a pair of white panties between his mattress and the bed frame. I left them there."

"Are they stained, bloodied?"

"I didn't look that closely."

In their circuit around the ward, they wove in and out between their fellow lunatics, as if imbedding them in a magic tapestry.

As part of the ground crew, Snow raked the lawn. He raked the gravel drive and he raked the gardens. He knew the function of the instrument in his hands, so he went on raking, drawing its tines across gravel and grass alike. He watched the others to get the pace and rhythm of it and then, bending slightly over the handle, made changes in the surface patterns of his earthly canvas. Under the late morning sun he was mesmerized by the movement of his rake against the sameness of the green. It was good to be outside. The freshness of the air was almost palpable with its lingering saltwater scents. Each blade of grass stood out against its background, clipped tops, ragged curl, viridian. Newly mown it offered to Snow the heady musk of sex. He took off his shirt, baring his white chest and shoulders to the late summer sun.

He raked slowly toward the large trees to the north side of West Lawn, aimlessly, but strangely satisfied by the motion alone. He floated with the sun and the movement, feeling suspended in time, part of a surreal landscape. It's possible he thought, to be, just to be, in an asylum. I rake, therefore I am. I rake because I've been told to, but it's comforting to do what one is told to do, mindlessly, letting the world come to me. The sun is real the grass is real the trees... He looked up at the towering Douglas fir and hemlock and saw them for a moment the way Emily Carr must have seen them, growing in

shadowed spirals toward the heavens, their rooted talons holding the
fragile earth in orbit.

And then, just as quickly, the feeling was gone. The sun became
too hot on his shoulders; his muscles tired and the click in his left hip
began to annoy him. This pointless exercise irritated him. His hands
threatened to blister on the tool's handle. So suddenly it all changed.
His moment of peace, once examined and savored, vanished, and
again he felt unsure. How is a man to live today?

He leaned on his rake to rest a minute, a little light-headed from
the physical exertion and the brightness of the sun in his eyes. There
hadn't been a single thing he had done since his childhood when he
had not, part of the time, wondered whether he might be better off
doing something else. Working, studying, resting, vacationing,
playing, parenting, drinking, even loving. No, there had been a few
moments of sex when he had simply participated without the off-
screen commentary droning in his ear.

Snow returned to his raking in the shadow of a large cedar tree.
He noted the simple pleasure of finding shade from the burning sun,
his emotions bouncing back again. Well, maybe it wasn't so
complicated after all. Just Brennan's antidepressant medication doing
its thing with his limbic system.

As he raked around the three-foot trunk his mind took him back
to his childhood. Large coniferous trees, red peeling arbutus, moss,
rock, shade. Thick pungent growth. Playing hide and seek, exploring,
building caverns in the undergrowth, climbing expeditions, searching
for butterflies and snakes, sitting for eternity in the arm of a tree or on
the soft moss carpet of a secret ledge, holding a girl's hand, watching
diamonds of sunlight sprinkle through the foliage.

"You can eat the roots y' know."

"You're kidding, you can't eat moss."

"Just the roots, not the green stuff. Here, try some of this."

"You go first."

"Like this, see. It tastes like liquorice."

"You'll get dirt in your mouth."

"It's just dirt. Nothing wrong with dirt."

A shadow moved in the woods and a slight blonde girl stepped
out from behind a tree, still in shadows. "Pssssst," she said.

"Is that you, Melanie?" asked Snow.

"It's me. Can you get away?"

Snow looked around at a man with a broom fifty yards away on his left, another with a rake on his right, each occupied. He felt foolish about his caution. This was not, after all, a road gang with an armed guard. He might be a patient but he was also a man. He took the rake with him and walked over to the shadows that held Melanie. She disappeared a little deeper into the woods and Snow followed. He came across her suddenly, sitting under a tree chewing a piece of grass. He sat against a tree opposite Melanie, pulling his shirt back on, fumbling with the buttons.

"He's in trouble," she said.

She was wearing jeans, sneakers, a T-shirt with no bra.

"Hardy?" There were fresh wounds on her forearms.

"Yes, Hardy."

"I know," he said.

"No. More than that. I don't mean the shoot-out on Granville Street. I mean now. He's been mugged, beaten up. He's hiding out on Wreck Beach."

"How do you know all this?"

"He phoned me. From a telephone booth."

"He should give himself up," said Snow.

"I think he's hurt. He was coughing and things. And I don't think he has anything to eat."

"Why are you telling me this?"

"You're his friend too," said Melanie.

For a moment Snow pondered that statement. "How do you propose we help him?"

"He needs me," said Melanie. "I must go to him."

"You can't help him. He's got to give himself up."

"He needs me and nothing can stop me going to him." She spoke with defiance but quickly cast her eyes down and said, in a different mood, "It's just that..."

"Just what?"

"It doesn't matter, not really." She began to pick herself up.

"Come on," said Snow. "Tell me." He didn't want her to leave.

"I thought..." she said, looking up at Snow's eyes. "I thought maybe you would come too. He might listen to you. You could make him go to a hospital."

"Melanie, I'm locked up in here at night."

"That's no problem," said Melanie. "Just ask Victor. He has keys."

"He doesn't have a key to the door of the ward."

"Yes he does. He has keys to everything. He always does."

"But he never said... He's never used them."

"He just has them is all I know. Hardy told me. Ask him."

"Okay, suppose Karpov has a key and we get out of here tonight, what then?"

"We can hitchhike into Vancouver."

"Nobody'll pick up two hitchhikers outside the gates of Essondale in the middle of the night."

"We'll steal a car then. One way or the other we'll get there."

"I don't know how to steal a car."

"Well I do," said Melanie. "Hardy showed me how one time. I know how to do it."

Snow had no answer. He brushed a fly away and shifted his position. There was coolness in the woods away from the sun. He looked up at the branches above him, blinking when the sun exploded through the leaves. "You shouldn't be in the woods alone."

"I'm okay."

"I mean with what happened to Jeanie."

"It wasn't Matthew."

"Well, whoever it was."

"You'll help us, won't you, Dr. Snow?"

When Snow arrived back on the ward after his day of raking, he paused at the door and watched Karpov for a moment. Karpov looked up, saw Snow, and began the shrugging, stretching, wriggling movements that Snow had come to see as expressions of anticipation and pleasure. At that moment his face was receptive and open, even eager, but by the time Snow had walked the distance between them; Karpov had it all under control. He thrust a hand out as if to salute Snow, rested it on the arm of his wheelchair, then began to speak as if no time had passed since he had last talked with his friend. "I was wrong before. When Malraux said, 'A man is good for nothing but to die when there is nothing left of his childhood, nor of his adolescence,' he did not mean that a man should stop living. There is a vast difference, my friend, between dying and not living."

"How have you been today?" asked Snow. "You should try to come outside. See if they'll let you."

"I am quite well here. What better place to study human destiny?"

"It was good to be outside," said Snow. "I felt almost human for the first time in many months."

"Perhaps for a moment the wind, the sun and the rustle of leaves can make man forget his own death. But only for a moment. It is all too clear that the sun and the wind will remain long after we have gone. Do you think it is possible, Robert, to envy moving air and sunlight?"

"They're not alive."

"Like you and I?"

"Like you and me."

"Surely then, they can hold no particular meaning for our existence. Man cannot conquer death by sunbathing. He can only hide in an idea, or lovemaking, or opiates. Perhaps even in war. Is it not ironic, Robert, that man seeks immortality through warfare? The act of killing is God making."

"So killing Jeanie was God making for someone?"

"Well, it may have been the motivation."

"The others are gathering for supper now, Victor."

"I will walk on my sticks if you help me."

Snow picked up two aluminium crutches from the floor beside the wheelchair and handed them to Karpov. The Bulgarian struggled to strap them around his upper arms, and then, the crutches lying at right angles on either side of his chair like oars, made ready to extricate himself. "Malraux is a good example," he said, "a very good example." Sweat began to form on his brow. His face grew red as he edged toward the front of his chair, placed his hands on the plastic arms, pushed down, lifting his body a few inches off the seat.

For the first time Snow noticed the clumsiness in Karpov's hands and was awed by the effort the man expended in the simple act of standing. "He was born...into the existential tradition of Sartre and Camus. He believed at first that man's death is his only certainty and therefore his only true motivator." He wriggled his feet in under his center of gravity, pulled his oars in to his side one at a time, and with another push with his hands and an intake of breath, separated himself from the wheelchair held steady by Snow. "Of course he was also a communist." Karpov took a hesitant step forward. "He believed that man's nature could be changed by altering his social system. If you allow man dignity he becomes...good. He also said that dignity is founded on suffering. I believe the man was quite confused." He threw his right leg forward by swinging it at the hip, dragging his foot behind, adjusting his crutches, pulling his left leg even, thighs quivering with the effort. "Late in life he devoted his time to the study of art and genius. He gave up on ordinary man, you see."

Snow walked beside him, uncertain how much to help as Karpov laboriously placed one crutch in front of the other, dragging his legs even with them, his body twisting grotesquely as it followed. It was clear to Snow that Karpov was half a person, physically, and that his bottom, dead half was a great burden to his top half. It was a shame his legs could not be discarded like the appendages of an octopus or the shell of a snail.

Snow helped Karpov into a chair in the dining area, opposite an old Down's Syndrome, beside the man who rocked all day, even as he sat, still thrusting his pelvis in and out. The smell of cabbage, always present, was stronger now, the room hot and close.

"Schopenhauer said that the will is the strong blind man who carries on his shoulders the lame man who can see."

"You and I, Victor?" Without waiting for an answer Snow went off to load a tray for the two of them.

When Snow returned Karpov continued talking between mouthfuls. "Modern life has destroyed our rhythms, the natural oscillations of life. We have placed between ourselves and the earth's crust a multitude of systems, schedules, rituals and materials. Did you ever notice, Robert, in this place, in this madhouse, the inmates have either lost the capacity for rhythm, or they have been taken over, like the man next to me, by an artificial rhythm, what the doctors call a side effect."

"Scuse me," said the rocking man, his voice coming out in synchrony with his pelvic thrusts. "Could you...pass the...salt...please." And after he had salted the scraps on his plate, he said, "Do you...know...where I might...meet...a...young girl?"

"It is a noble profession," said Karpov, "procuring. And a dream as good as any other." But the rocking man had turned back to his food.

"Victor, do you have a key?"

"A key, Robert? I have many keys."

"A key to the ward. Melanie tells me you have a key to the ward." Karpov looked for a moment like a man who had been caught in a lie.

"Yes, Robert, I carry a key, like every other madman in this place. The difference is that my key will unlock the door while their keys will only unlock some imagined boundary to their will. I don't know which is better. Why do you want it, Robert?"

"I...it's a crazy idea, Victor."

"Ideas are not crazy, only the fools who believe in them."

"Hardy is hiding out and Melanie says he's hurt. She wants to help him."

"And so...?"

"She wants me to help her find him tonight. She plans to steal a car and drive into Vancouver."

"Ah...Matthew. The soldier of fortune is injured on the battlefield and his lady rushes to his side. Where do you fit in, Robert?"

"She said I'm one of his friends."

"In that case I go too."

"Victor, we can't take you."

"No Karpov, no key."

"How do I get you down the stairs?"

"We'll use the elevator," said Karpov.

"It'll wake the whole building."

"In that case you can carry me, Robert. I weigh very little. You can make a second trip for my chair."

"But Victor..."

"If you want the key."

Snow was looking at Karpov and thinking about this when the savant came over suddenly toward them, passed them, then came back again, pacing angrily. "Thieves!" he announced.

"What?" asked Snow.

"It's gone."

"What's gone?"

"You know," said the savant, and then walked away to stand in a far corner, looking at them.

"Victor. I thought you left them."

"I did, Robert. I did."

"Maybe someone was watching when you found them."

"Have you told Brennan yet?"

"I didn't get a chance. Figured I'd have to leave her a note. Why are we getting into the middle of this, Victor?"

"It is human to do so," said Karpov.

"Victor, for once why can't you just say something simple and clear, like, 'Because we're fucking nuts'?"

THIRTY

Late that night, between the nursing supervisor's regular ward rounds, Snow wheeled Karpov across the wooden floor of the ward. He knew the others were watching from their beds. No matter how drugged, tired and senseless they were, they would be watching in the dark, recording his actions. They would make no sounds, no judgements now, but tomorrow they would tell their stories, perhaps in rhymes and riddles.

The key Karpov selected from his chain unlocked the door, and the cripple and the blind man left their fellows behind. In the corridor Snow whispered, "Your chair needs oiling." Every sound seemed to reverberate off the barren walls. Under the red glow from the exit sign, Karpov's eyes shone with a surprising eagerness. "A man of both intellect and action," he said, as if rehearsing his own press release.

"How do I carry you?"

"Your arm here, under my legs. The other under my arm."

"Here. I've got it...just a minute, uhhh. What about the chair?"

"Push it against the wall. No one sees an empty wheelchair in the hospital."

Snow manoeuvred the door open with his foot and carried Karpov to the head of the stairs. Karpov's body was strangely inflexible.

"My tobacco. Get my tobacco, Robert."

Snow carried him back through the door and held him within reach of his pouch and then returned to the head of the stairs. He was a little more careless this time and the door closed behind them with an ominous thud. The threat of discovery grew in Snow; he could taste bile in his throat. He took a careful step forward, felt his way down the first stair, leaning against the railing for balance. "Don't look back, Orpheus," said Karpov. He had a sweetish smell about him.

Snow struggled down a dozen steps to the landing. Here he paused to catch his breath, leaned back against a wall, and, ignoring Karpov's injunction, looked back up to the door at the head of the stairs. Beyond he could hear the unmistakable rhythmic clomp of the night supervisor walking the corridor. She passed by the door and the abandoned wheelchair.

Snow's arms were tired. "I'll have to try it another way," he whispered. Before Karpov could protest he threw him sack-like over his right shoulder, catching him behind the knees. Now, left hand free to guide him on the railing, he made better progress down the second flight. At the bottom he propped Karpov against the wall as one might a straw-filled doll, paused to catch his breath, and climbed back up the stairs to retrieve the wheelchair. Snow pushed the door open onto a once again deserted corridor. He pulled Karpov's wheelchair to the head of the stairs and carried it down. It seemed for a moment as if he were reassembling two cruelly separated halves into one useful unit.

"Ah, my chariot. Thank you, Robert."

Once in his chair, Karpov become whole. He lifted his legs at the calf and placed his feet on the runners. With Snow pushing, they passed through a door into the main hall, illuminated like the one above by a red exit sign.

At the end of the corridor they found a fire exit, with crash bars locked only from the outside.

"It isn't wired," said Karpov, reading Snow's concern about alarms.

 Snow put his back to the bars and the doors swung open. "Quickly."

Karpov was busy trying to light a cigarette and the breeze from outside was frustrating his efforts.

"Close the door for a minute. I can't get...the thing started."

"We don't have time for that, Victor. Come on." He pulled Karpov out backwards and suddenly feeling the night chill, asked, "Where's your sweater?"

"I also forgot my bottle," said Karpov.

"Your what?"

"My bottle. You'll have to help me when it's time to piss."

Like ghostly shadows they were sliding down the pathway toward the back of the admission wing. The night was dark and moonless, and a cool September breeze washed away the smell and taste of the institution.

On the other side of the building they found the parking lot, empty now, save for a few cars belonging to the night staff. Melanie was waiting for them. "I almost gave up on you," she said. Karpov's cigarette glowed in the dark.

"What now?"

"This one," said Melanie. "It's Dr. Brennan's. She's on call tonight. That means she won't be leaving the hospital until five tomorrow afternoon. The others get off at seven in the morning." She'd already got the door open.

"Very clever," said Karpov.

"And if she catches us she won't lay charges. She's kind of a bleeding heart."

Snow wondered if this was the same young girl who took overdoses, waited vaguely in life for instructions from others, and usually didn't seem to know her own mind. He decided it was the same person, just a different script writer for the moment. This can't last, he thought. He slid Karpov into the back seat of Marjorie Brennan's Toyota, pushing aside a child's safety chair and a soft woollen sweater. It was then that he felt he had violated her in some way. He folded Karpov's chair and tried to put it in the trunk. It didn't fit.

"Leave it," said Karpov. "Leave it in the parking space."

In the front seat Melanie bent under the dashboard and fiddled with some wires. The car sputtered to life. "See," she said. "I told you I could do it. You have to drive, Dr. Snow."

"Me?"

"I can't drive. I don't have my license."

Marjorie stretched out on the bed in the duty doctor's room and tried to concentrate her mind on the television screen. She had considered paying an evening visit to each ward but thinking of the veiled hostility with which the nurses would greet her, dismissed the idea. At night the wards belonged to them, the patients were theirs. Ultimate authority resided with the night supervisor and the nurses generally resented the intrusion of overly conscientious doctors. Especially, thought Marjorie, women doctors.

To be on call for the whole complex was at once a boring and intimidating experience. Intimidating because anything was possible: murder, rape, suicide, psychosis, death, violence; boring because seldom did anything happen. The calls she got were usually requests to re-order medication. Or to fill out and sign certification or return orders.

She switched off the television and turned her attention to the small shelf of books and magazines. She tried Friedman and Kaplan at first and then a small book called Schizophrenia in Focus, but found she could not concentrate on either. There was always a foreboding quality to the asylum at night and the duty doctor's room was a poorly ventilated closet. She could feel the institution around and above her, pushing on the walls. There was also a Spartan, masculine tone to the room (and a small pile of Penthouse magazines) which left her feeling uncomfortable.

With nothing else to do she pondered herself in the bathroom mirror, looking first at her teeth and then at new wrinkles on her neck, comparing herself unfavourably to the June centerfold. When the phone rang she started, as if caught in an act of shameful vanity.

"Dr. Brennan?"

"Yes, Dr. Brennan here."

"This is Two East calling. We have a patient, a Mr. Friedlich. He's quite agitated."

Marjorie waited for the nurse to carry on, but she said nothing further.

"Is he a new patient?"

"No. We've had him for several months now."

"What's his diagnosis?"

"Just a minute. Here it is. Paranoid. He's a paranoid."

"How old is the man?"

"Just a minute. Uhhh, fifty-two."

"Did anything upset him today?"

"I don't know. I just came on duty."

"What medication is he on?"

"Haldol ten milligrams q.i.d. and twenty milligrams p.r.n."

"Have you given him the extra twenty milligrams?"

"No. The order ran out yesterday."

"Oh."

"Pardon me?"

"I just said oh. Is it a p.r.n. order that you're after?"

"That's up to you, doctor."

"I know. But did you want me to see him or were you just requesting some sedation for the night?"

"You can see him if you wish."

"Look, how agitated is he?"

"He's okay now. We're just afraid we won't be able to get him to stay in bed tonight."

"You just want an order in case. I see. Okay. Do you prefer nozinan or chlorpromazine for p.r.n. sedation?"

"You're the doctor."

"Okay. Then how about 100 milligrams of chlorpromazine p.r.n.?"

"Dr. Humphrey always uses nozinan on this ward."

"All right. All right. Nozinan it is. Fifty milligrams. Are you happy with that?"

"Thank you, doctor."

Marjorie hung up the phone and paced. Christ, what an inane conversation. That passive-aggressive bitch got her to do exactly what she wanted in the first place without giving her any information and without taking any responsibility. She was still pacing and ranting about nurse-doctor games when the telephone rang again.

"Dr. Brennan?"

"Yes."

"We have a patient missing on Three West. I think you know her, Melanie Williams."

"How long now?"

"She should have been back on the ward by nine but we gave her a couple more hours. Maybe two hours now."

"She's voluntary?"

"Uh huh. I wouldn't be worried except for this thing happened to Jeanie."

"I understand. Have you called her mother?"

"Not yet."

"That's about all we can do now. See if she's reached home and have her mother call us if she arrives."

Driving the stolen car along Highway 1 down the Fraser Valley toward Vancouver with Melanie in the seat beside him and Victor Karpov in the back seat, Snow rolled the window down and took a deep breath of the passing night air. It contained the crackle of early autumn and the flickering of insects soon to perish. Snow found the night drive exhilarating and for a moment he wished he were alone. Then Melanie leaned into his shoulder and Karpov, quite excited now, began to talk. Snow didn't hear the words so much as the rhythms and cadences of Karpov's voice. He let them soothe him and he let himself enjoy the delicious contrast between Melanie's warm body on his right and the cool night air on his left.

"There are those who believe the self and the universe can be found in contemplation," announced Karpov. "'The mind of the sage in repose becomes the mirror of the universe'". He coughed and Snow heard him trying to pull himself forward in the seat.

"Why don't you put that sweater on, Victor? The one in the back seat?"

Karpov struggled to pull it over his shoulders. "To go somewhere is interesting. To leave someplace is exciting. To escape is sexy. And one's destination proves a greater or lesser disappointment in direct proportion," he said.

"This may not end very well for any of us," said Snow.

"What, Robert?" He hadn't heard him above the wind from the open window, and the sweater bunched around his ears.

"I said this might not end very well for any of us."

"Only by avoiding beginnings can we escape endings. Could you roll up the window, Robert?" He pulled the sweater down around his chest.

When Snow rolled up the window, Melanie's left hand dropped in his lap, on his right thigh. He took her hand in his. He was father to her, or big brother. But she wasn't his, she wasn't anybody's. She didn't even seem to belong to herself. He stopped himself from thinking and went back to listening to Karpov's mesmerizing voice.

When they came to the outskirts of Vancouver, Melanie roused herself to give directions. Snow came off the highway onto East Broadway and drove across town. It was two a.m. already and with the slower traffic, store fronts and deserted sidewalks, he became acutely aware of being in a precarious position. When a patrol car passed he felt the fugitive's tremor of excitement. Melanie directed them across Vancouver and through a large residential area to the wooded lands of the University endowment. After ten miles of densely populated suburb they were suddenly on a lonely forested road winding toward the coast.

"Are you sure about this?" asked Snow.

"I'm certain," said Melanie. "We used to hitchhike out here a lot." And then, as if it were an explanation, "There's nude sunbathing here."

On Marine Drive, Snow could only glimpse the ocean through the trees far down on his left, but he sensed its presence fully. Melanie had him pull into an unmarked rest stop. There were no gates, no path, no signs visible in the narrow beam of headlights.

"It's over there," said Melanie, pointing across the road. "A steep path goes down to the beach. It's impossible to get down quietly, so it's where a lotta druggies hang out."

Snow could see the outlines of two cars parked along the edge of the road. He stalled the Toyota and then shut down its lights. After letting their eyes get accustomed to the dark, Snow and Melanie stepped out of the car.

"What about me?" Karpov asked.

"You'll have to wait here. It's too steep," said Melanie.

"Beware ye guilty souls. There lies the dismal shore of Acheron."

"We'll be careful," said Snow, understanding Karpov's meaning. Melanie led him across the highway to the edge of shadow and darkness. She found a path Snow couldn't see and, taking his hand in hers, began to feel her way down. Snow couldn't see his feet in the blackness. He automatically leaned backwards to balance and groped for footholds in the clay. The path was rough and steep, curving down to the beach a hundred feet below.

High above, Snow could see patches of sky behind thick cloud, but on either side, down, and straight ahead he could see nothing. Gravel slipped beneath his feet and rattled down the cliff. He could hear the ocean now, far below, through the thick brush. Melanie slipped and pulled on Snow's arm. He leaned back and held her while she scrambled to regain her footing. Then he took a step forward for better balance and suddenly there was no ground beneath him.

On her way to tend to the wounded head of an old man at the separate psycho geriatric unit called Forestview, Marjorie looked up the hill at the black forest edge and pictured first Jeanie dead and mutilated and then Melanie in Jeanie's place. She shuddered and walked on.

After assessing the old man's wound as a small three- suture cut, Marjorie's main concern became treating him quickly and getting away from Forestview before the smell of death and urine penetrated her clothing. She knew her woollen sweater could hold the odor for days. She cleaned his wound, draped the area with sterile cloth, and closed with black silk thread. At least the activity itself was satisfying. The old man muttered beneath the green drape on his face but made no attempt to pull it off. As she finished the nurse assisting her said, "Seeing as how you're already here, you might as well see Mr. Jones. We don't think he'll last the night."

Reluctantly Marjorie followed her to another bedside, deeper into the ammonia-ripe atmosphere, farther away from the door and fresh air. They were being thoughtful, she knew, for if the man did die tonight it would be much easier to fill out the death certificate if she had seen him alive.

On the bed lay an older man with Down's Syndrome, hot, breathing with difficulty, comatose. He looked 60, 70, but Marjorie knew he might be 30 or 40 for people with Down's age poorly and the pallor of sickness could add another ten years. He has pneumonia, said one of the nurses. I can see that, said Marjorie. What is he being treated with? Nothing, said the nurse. Just fluids. Is anything else the matter with him? Dr. Brennan asked, while she examined his chest with the ward stethoscope. They watched her intently. Pneumonia. People don't die from pneumonia anymore. Why isn't he on antibiotics?

Back in the nursing office Marjorie thumbed through the man's chart. There wasn't much information available. His first name was Herman. He was forty-four years old, admitted to Forestview five years ago after living for a while with his brother's family. His IQ was below fifty, he had cataracts on both eyes, and he was prone to respiratory infections. Gaps of eight months passed without a single note written by any attending physician and when she did find a note it summarized his attributes in a few indecipherable initials such as PERLA and AP/Lat. neg.

Six weeks ago, Marjorie learned, his chest x-ray had shown bilateral pneumonia and he had been put on Ampicillin. A week later, when he showed little improvement, he had been switched to Tetracycline, and a week after that, Amoxicillin. Then the medication

146

orders stopped and the notes indicated the presence of creps, rales, and rhonchi in the man's lungs without mentioning treatment.

Several doctors had seen Herman Jones. Each had noted his findings and prescribed nothing. They had decided to let him die. Decided wasn't exactly the word for it, because nowhere on the chart did it say what they were doing and Marjorie knew the chance of several duty doctors getting together to discuss the case was practically nil. They were letting him die by default.

The issue wasn't clear in her mind. Perhaps they knew better than she. Perhaps his life was miserable at the best of times; perhaps he was dying from other diseases as well. Would she like to be kept alive as an invalid, an institutionalised mental defective, a middle-aged mental defective? She looked at the nurses, but received no clues from their expressions of studied indifference. "What was he like?" She heard herself using the past tense.

"He was a management problem most of the time. Not since he's been sick, of course."

"Has he any family?"

"I haven't seen anyone visit."

Marjorie went back and examined Herman Jones once more. With her thumb and index finger she squeezed him hard at the base of his nose between his epicanthic eyes. He moaned and tried to roll away from the pain. It was a test for deep sensation, a way of gauging the coma, but Marjorie, having done it, wondered of its necessity. For surely she had already made up her mind to go along. To treat him now he would have to be transferred to an intensive-care unit, and nobody, but nobody, would appreciate that.

Anyhow, it was too late. The man would die no matter what. Several male doctors had decided to stop treatment and now if she came along, a woman, and tried to rescue this patient...emotional woman, unable to detach. Well, after the episode with Hardy she might have to agree with them. What the hell was she thinking when she delivered the clothes?

On her way back to the nursing office, she let her mind write the kind of black biography that might justify her lack of action. Herman Jones, imbecile, epileptic, abandoned by his family, chronically depressed, at times suicidal, congenital problems with his heart and gastrointestinal system, practically blind, only a few more years to live, friendless, chronic respiratory disease. As she enlarged the list she found that there was little short of death that justified death. It was one thing to pull the plug on a life-support system, it was another to withhold such a simple treatment as antibiotic therapy.

In the nursing office she added a cryptic note to the bottom of the last page and then, pausing over the doctors' order sheet, made up her mind and wrote down a small list. Looking over Marjorie's shoulder one of the nurses said, "We'll have to transfer him for that."

"No we won't. We can do it right here. Get the I.V. stand and a bottle of Ringer's."

Back at the bedside Marjorie started the intravenous drip, injected some antibiotic directly into the tubing and established an oxygen mask on Mr. Jones' face. She was sure, as were the nurses, that it was a futile gesture, but she felt better having done it. "Call me if there's any change," she said.

Snow fell straight down, six feet, ten feet, twelve feet, grasping in the darkness for purchase in the sandy cliff edge. The two or three seconds it took to fall gave him time to imagine himself plunging to a rocky shore below, and time to think, "My body's too old for this." He landed with a thud in some brush against the trunk of a large tree, his breath and senses knocked from his body. He lay there for a moment, unsure what had happened, the darkness suddenly oppressive. Straining his neck around, he searched for sky and, finding it on his third try, was greatly relieved to see light patches lending dimension to his inky void. He rested for a moment now, waiting for his wind and the feeling in his body to return. He moved each limb a little and found nothing broken or paralysed.

"Melanie." No answer.

"Melanie!" he shouted.

He thought she might have fallen as well, but he couldn't recall hearing her call out. She couldn't be that far away.

"Melanie, are you all right?" No answer. The sea was louder now, rolling pebbles up and down the shore, slapping against rock faces and curling up the beach. Snow pulled himself to his hands and knees and began to crawl sideways and downward toward the sound of the water. He found what he thought was the path again and slid down it backwards, calling now and then for Melanie.

At the end of the path he stood up and looked westward. Far ahead he could see a faint horizon, but nothing was visible at his feet. On his left he sensed a mass that had to be a rock promontory and on his right he could hear waves washing on a sandy beach. Turning back he confronted total darkness, a wall, a cliff of gravel and trees. Without caution now he called for Melanie, but his voice was a small thing in the darkness. He considered climbing back to look for her but for a moment his present experience stopped him.

There can be no other place, he thought, that holds for man such awareness of his own frailty: the bottom of a great cliff, the ocean's edge at his feet, and all in darkness. And yet standing there feeling vulnerable, Snow could also sense a share in the power surrounding him. Water shifting in the blackness. The smell of salt, seaweed, and cedar. A cold wind beginning to cut through his shirt. A high breaking wave stinging him with its spray.

Snow was jolted out of his reverie by small animal noises coming from some feet away on the beach. He thought of Melanie injured and began to walk in the direction of the sounds. He called out once but the noises stopped and he waited for them to begin again. Stumbling on a rock he dropped to his knees in the sand and crawled toward the plaintive cries, feeling his way among the pebbles. A wave caught his left ankle like a giant cold hand. He crawled higher on the beach to dry sand and reeds. The sound was closer now, and confusing. Straight ahead a moving shape became visible against the ebony forest. Snow reached out to touch it: a boot, then flesh, a bony eminence, movement...

"What the fuck you doing?"

It was Hardy's voice and beneath it Melanie's laughter.

"Are you all right?"

Melanie giggled.

"Christ almighty!" said Snow. "I thought you were hurt, here you are fucking. Christ. I don't believe it." He rolled onto his back looking up at the sky. "I could have been lying a few feet away dead or injured with the two of you making out in the sand."

"I'm sorry, Dr. Snow," said Melanie. "But he wanted me so badly."

When his surprise had worn off and the tension had left his body Snow chuckled at the sky and then said, "So, Melanie, how is he?"

But they were going at it once more and she didn't answer. He can't be that badly beaten up, thought Snow.

When the scuffing in the sand stopped, Hardy said, "I'm okay, man. Just a few bruises is all." He stood up, silhouetted against the horizon, naked except for pants bunched at his ankles, and began to pull his clothes back on.

"Where the fuck is my sweater? It's colder than a nun's tit." He pulled his pants up and fastened the buckle. Melanie felt around in the sand and handed Hardy a shirt and sweater.

"I can't find my panties. Wha'd'ya do with my panties?" Snow could see her shadow wriggling into a T shirt, and then pulling up her jeans. "Oh God," she said. "I've got sand in my crotch."

"Lessee," said Hardy, sliding a hand down her jeans.

Melanie pulled the hand out and stepped away. "It's starting to get light, we have to go."

"Where to? Where do we take him?"

"He's coming with us, Dr. Snow, back to Essondale."

"Good. It's the only way, Matthew. Give yourself up now. The longer you're on the run the more dangerous it gets."

"Wait a minute. Just wait a fucking minute. I'm not giving myself up. No way, man. I'm just coming to the grounds like Melanie says. I can camp out there."

"It's the last place they'd look for him, Dr. Snow. It's perfect. We can sneak him food and things."

"On the grounds? Camping? At Essondale?"

"That's right."

"You're both crazy."

"They'll never think of it, Dr. Snow."

"You couldn't do it very long."

"Just so's it cools off a bit. Then I'll go. Maybe down to the Dakotas for a while."

Snow suddenly realized that Hardy's imagery came directly from comic books, film and T.V. He could understand life when it was drawn boldly and simply. His mind, like Melanie's, was cluttered with mass-produced symbols. "This is very crazy, but all right. I guess it's as good a plan as any. If either of you know the way back we should go."

"I know the path," said Hardy. "Just follow me." He took Melanie's hand and she in turn took Snow's and the cowboy led them in the darkness back to the foot of the rough clay path winding through the trees up the side of the cliff. Hardy dug in his boots and pulled them up the slope. Halfway up, Snow called for a break, and the three sat for a moment breathing heavily, bodies touching in the dark.

At the top they crouched in the brush for a moment to let the light of a south bound van go past and then they crossed the street to their car.

"Couldn't you do any better than that?" said Hardy, when he saw they were heading for the small Toyota.

"It's Dr. Brennan's car."

"Matthew, is that you in the turgid darkness?"

"Karpov. They didn't tell me they brought you along."

"It is of no consequence. I am but a witness to this night's folly."

"How are you?"

"Surviving. No more. It is my animal destiny. The one instinct not yet sullied by civilization."

"We should go," said Snow, looking up and down the highway. "A patrol car is bound to come by."

This time Hardy hot wired the engine and then climbed into the back seat with Karpov. Melanie started to follow when Snow said, "It'll look strange, three in the back, and one in the front."

"It's okay. You can ride in front with Mr. Snow, Mel."

With the car doors open, the interior lights shone on Hardy's face for a moment. He turned away but not before Snow had seen the dark discoloration on his cheek, the crusted wound over his left temple and the deep set tiredness of his eyes. "You were pretty badly beaten up."

"Not so bad. I'll survive."

Karpov said, "Ah, you see, we are all survivors. We are not much to look at and most would not envy our circumstances, but we are all survivors."

At two A.M. they called from West Lawn to let Marjorie know that two patients were missing, Robert Snow and Victor Karpov. It was the supervisor. Should we send out an order for return? Marjorie rubbed her face, pulled herself awake, and answered, "No."

"They were involuntary, both of them."

"I know that."

"The policy..."

"Forget the policy on this one. It might be the best thing for both of them."

"You're the doctor."

"I'll come over in the morning and write something to cover you, okay?"

She fell back asleep wondering what the hell they were up to and what the hell she was doing covering for them.

When they had settled in, Snow turned the car onto Marine Drive and began to trace his path back to Essondale. His watch read five-thirty which meant it would be getting light when they reached the asylum. Once again Melanie curled into his shoulder. At first Snow instinctively edged away, sensing Hardy's eyes on the back of his neck. But the only noise that came from the back seat was Karpov's continuing discourse on the nature of will and so Snow relaxed and let Melanie's head drift to his chest.

"We are passing through a very difficult period of philosophical thought," said Karpov. "The world is being pulled, kicking and screaming, into the 21st century. The Moslems drag their 13th century heels, Christians yearn for the simplicity of the 19th century, Jews build fortresses. They are all resisting the expansion of our consciousness, the breaking down of old boundaries. This is not, of course, unique in history." There was a pause while Karpov fiddled with his tobacco. Snow turned left on McDonald and headed north. "Many years ago the battle was fought between the idea of man ruled by supernatural forces, and enlightened man, reasoning man. With Freud and Darwin, instinctual man reared his head and engaged in a bloody struggle with religious man. There are those who claim that man has choices; his essence is his consciousness. And there are still others who claim that man's consciousness is irrelevant, immaterial, an illusion. Would you roll up your window, Robert, so that I may light this cigarette?" A match flared in the back seat.

"So, which do you believe, Victor?" asked Snow.

"None."

"None?"

"No, you see Robert, to believe in any one idea of man would be a mistake. Any single answer can lead to fascism."

Snow had learned to let Karpov's words sift through his consciousness like gravel in a gold miner's pan. Occasionally he stopped to examine a sparkle that caught his mind's eye amidst the worthless pebbles. He was driving on Broadway now, two sentences behind Karpov, thinking about his own indecisiveness, when he heard Hardy say, "Food".

Up ahead on his right Snow saw the sign that had caught the cowboy's attention. An all night restaurant. Open 24 hours. Melanie roused herself, "Oh, let's stop for something to eat."

"It might not be safe to stop."

"Just bring me a couple hamburgers. I'll stay in the car."

After Snow pulled into the parking area it was decided that he and Melanie would bring hamburgers to the car. They pooled their money and came up with eleven dollars. Like most all night roadhouses there was a certain comforting loneliness to the place. A place that did not intrude as it let you know that you were not the only one seeking food and warmth in the middle of the night. They brought back a small box of wrapped hamburgers, packages of salt, ketchup and napkins. Snow took a large bite from his burger before steering the car east on Broadway. It tasted as good as any he had ever eaten before, though he knew it was really a poor, massed produced, soy-extended facsimile of the real thing.

Hardy ate like a man who hadn't eaten in several days. Melanie took time to add ketchup and salt, and Karpov continued to talk though his mouth was full. With food in his stomach, the gray light of dawn before him, the blonde child-woman once more snuggled into his shoulders, and his two friends in the back seat, Snow experienced a brief flush of well being. He was driving back to an insane asylum, the funny farm, a mental hospital, and yet he felt good. In fact he had a disquieting sense of coming home. On the beach, for a moment, he had been gripped by agoraphobia and now the walls of Essondale seemed comforting. He reflected on his friends - a mad, crippled philosopher, a cowboy driven by an unrelenting demon, and a young girl taken too early from the mould, still seeking definition. Karpov was talking on as if to the rhythm of the tires on the pavement, something now about the conspiracy of Locke, Watson, Skinner and someone called Gumplowicz to shape the nature of man to suit the needs of society's technology. "We are already preparing ourselves for robot masters," he said.

The cowboy sat quietly. With a passing car from the opposite direction Snow could see the reflection of his face in the rear view mirror. Hardy's deep set eyes appeared sightless, the energy drained from his body. For the moment he was spent.

The sun was just rising when Snow pulled into the parking lot of Essondale. This time he reached under the dash himself to separate the ignition wires. Melanie had been sitting up since they had passed through the asylum's great stone gate and Karpov had fallen silent.

"My wheelchair is still there. We have not been discovered."

"How will we get back in?"

"There is no problem getting into a mental hospital, Robert, only getting out."

"He's right," said Melanie. "Just go up and knock. They'll let you in."

"What about Hardy?"

"You take him with you, Dr. Snow, up to the woods behind West Lawn. He knows where to go."

"I have to ask, Matthew? Did you have anything to do with Jeanie's death?"

"No, man. Christ no."

"Okay. You sure you're up to this?"

"I'm fine. I'm okay." In the light of early dawn Snow could see Hardy calling on his reserves of strength, tightening his body and wriggling his toes in his high leather boots.

"I'll bring you blankets and food later today," said Melanie. She turned and walked toward the steps of the admission wing. In the faint light, Snow thought he saw her body and posture change. As she climbed the steps her shoulders slumped and her walk lost its fluidity. He wondered if her face took on its practiced look of vacant melancholia.

With Hardy's help Snow pulled Karpov from the back seat of the Toyota and carried him to the wheelchair. Once settled there, Karpov resumed his talk and rolled another cigarette from his pouch of makings. Snow looked at his watch; they were just minutes ahead of the arrival of the early morning shift. Hardy and Snow took turns pushing Karpov up the black pathway to West Lawn. Once there Hardy left them and headed for the woods alone. Snow turned the chair, pushing Karpov in the direction of the side door from which they had exited some hours before.

"No, wait," said Karpov. "We must return through the front door. It will look more innocent. And this time we will use the elevator."

At five in the morning Forestview called to announce that Mr. Herman Jones had ceased to breathe. She got up immediately, knowing if she didn't that she was liable to next wake up around noon, took her time struggling into her clothes and dropped Murine into her eyes to reduce their itchiness.

On the ward she examined the body, now lying in repose, peaceful, and to some extent already tidied up. The nursing aides had shaved his stubbly beard and stuffed cotton in his cheeks to obliterate the unsightly hollowness of death. They had tended to him well in death. In the chart, Marjorie made her notation: Pronounced dead, 6 a.m. - and she filled out the death certificate. She was about to leave when one of the nurses pushed a piece of paper across the desk.

"What's this?"

"Phone number of the next of kin."

"And?"

"You're supposed to call. They like to hear it from the doctor."

"Whose phone number is it?"

"I think it's his brother. He has the same last name."

Marjorie fumbled with the paper for a moment, thinking, at least they'll be prepared. Dr. Sweeney must have talked to them within the past week. I'm sure they'll be relieved if anything. She summoned her courage and dialled the number from the piece of paper.

A woman answered.

"Is that Mrs. Jones?"

"Yes."

"Could I speak with your husband please.?"

"Who's calling?"

"It's Dr. Brennan, from the hospital. About your brother-in-law."

"Herman? Something's happened to Herman? I'll get him right away."

Marjorie could hear them in the background: "Wake up, Joe. It's the hospital. Something's happened to Herman."

"Oh God. Is he sick or something?"

"I don't know. She's waiting on the phone."

When Mr. Jones got himself to the telephone and Marjorie told him that his brother had died he sounded at first astonished, and then grief stricken. He covered up the mouthpiece with his hand and said to his wife, "Herman passed away in the night." And then to Dr. Brennan, "I don't understand, he was fine when we saw him last."

Marjorie grimaced.

"We were in just last week and he seemed fine. Course he had a bad cold and all but that was par for the course with Herman."

"It was a very bad strain of pneumonia," said Marjorie. That much was probably true.

"Just out of the blue like that. I don't understand it."

Marjorie didn't know what the hell to say to that. She was thinking Jesus Christ, doesn't anybody talk to families around here.

"We don't want an autopsy; he's been through enough in his lifetime."

"I understand," she said. "I won't press for a post mortem."

When Marjorie left the psychogeriatric ward that morning there was a bitter taste in her mouth and she was sure the smell of death would cling to her clothes all day. On her way back to the Admitting Wing she glanced up the hill and, in the early morning light, she saw Robert Snow hauling Victor Karpov and his wheelchair up the main steps of West Lawn. She looked at her watch. Quarter to seven. What the hell are they up to? She stood and watched until the two had negotiated the stairs and entered the main door. They were going in, not out. It didn't make sense. Where the hell had they been all night

Later that morning, after breakfast, rounds and conferencing with Dromore, Marjorie walked up the hill to West Lawn to see Robert Snow. Melanie had returned early in the morning, roughly the same time she'd seen Snow and Karpov return. The girl had asked to talk with Marjorie but Dromore had come by and said, "Melanie, Melanie, come along. Come and tell me where you've been all night."

Marjorie had said, "Maybe later," as Dromore led her away. On the way to West Lawn she didn't let herself ask why she wanted to see Robert Snow. She felt ill at ease, restless, adrift of her moorings. She didn't know what the hell was going on, here, at home, anywhere. But she had promised the supervisor she'd write something about not allowing an order for return.

Snow was asleep in a chair on the ward when Marjorie approached. Karpov was slumped in his wheelchair on the other side of the room. Snow started awake and rubbed his eyes.

Marjorie crossed her arms and stood in front of him. "You look better, considering."

"Considering what?"

"Being out all night."

"You know about that?"

"They asked me to send the police after you."

"Christ. That would have done it."

"What were you up to?"

Snow looked at her, said, "They took away my grounds privileges."

"Well, that's what they do."

"You know, Dr. Brennan, I think you were right about depression, affective disorder. I'm different now."

"Are they keeping you on antidepressants?"

"Can't you tell from my dry mouth?"

"So you want me to try to get you out of here, have a talk with Pawlitsky?"

Snow was surprised by a wave of anxiety. He said, "Yeah, sure.
The other thing you could do is write a nice letter I could take to the
College."

"So you're actually thinking of returning to life?"

"Maybe."

"Maybe?"

"Yeah."

"You didn't tell me what you were up to last night. You and
Karpov and Melanie."

Snow looked away from her eyes. "Remember I said there was an
idiot savant in here boasting about a pair of panties? Victor saw them,
says they're real and white. But they've disappeared."

"Disappeared?"

"Gone. He thinks we stole them."

"Is it worth getting the police to talk with this man?"

"He's crazy."

"Maybe a ward search."

"They still think Hardy did it?"

"I think so. I haven't heard them looking anywhere else."

"I don't think he did it."

"Who knows."

"Look, one other thing you could do for me."

"What?"

Snow had his hand on his face. He didn't answer for a moment,
and then said, "No, Christ. It's things I'll have to do myself."

"Okay. And you're not telling me about last night?"

"Maybe later."

In the afternoon Melanie opened another superficial wound on
her left forearm. Marjorie looked at it with a nurse in the clinic room.
Melanie, eyes on the floor, said, "Can I talk with you alone, Dr.
Brennan?"

The nurse looked at Marjorie. Marjorie nodded and the nurse left
the room. The room had an examining table, a sink and cabinets of
basic medical equipment. Marjorie sat in a chair opposite Melanie and
said, "Okay."

Melanie fidgeted. She played with her hands. She played with her
hair. She got up and paced. Tears formed in her eyes. Marjorie

expected a performance. Melanie sat down again and said, "I see Dr. Dromore, right?"

"Right."

"If I tell you something will you promise not to tell him?"

"I can't make that kind of promise."

"Well there's no point then." She got up and headed for the door.

"Wait a minute, Melanie. Sit down for a minute."

At the door Melanie said, "Just forget it."

"Melanie, listen for a minute. If it's something critical about Dr. Dromore, like you don't like him or something, I won't tell him. I promise. But if it's something else, like something from your past, he should know about it."

"You promise it's bad about Dromore you won't tell him?"

"I promise."

She stayed by the door and resumed playing with her hair.

Marjorie said, "How about this. Whatever it is, if I think Dromore should know I won't tell him, I'll ask you to tell him, okay?"

Melanie remained silent. Marjorie thought, Christ, I'm being sucked into some game here. But she decided to wait it out.

Melanie sat down. Looking at her feet she said, "Okay. It's like some stuff he does with me."

Over the next half hour, gently asking questions, Marjorie reverberated between disbelief, anger, disgust and horror. She didn't want to hear this. Christ, the child is psychotic. She manipulates and splits. She lies and fantasizes. Dromore is fucking brilliant. But brilliance had nothing to do with what she was hearing. And Melanie was telling it straight. Some tears and confusion but no histrionics, nothing excessive. Good Christ. She felt sick thinking about it. She stretched her legs out, sat silently for a few minutes. Melanie was saying, "He'll kill me he finds out I talked."

Marjorie leaned forward, pushed a Kleenex box in Melanie's direction, ironically remembering a sensitive interview she'd watched Dromore conduct, calling the young woman lass and offering her tissue. "Look, Melanie. I won't tell anybody about this. Let me think about it and talk with you some more."

"I see him tomorrow, in his office."

"Shit. Look, make yourself scarce. Just don't show up."

"He'll put me in seclusion."

"I know you're scared, but I'll make sure nothing happens. Give me some time to think about this. And Melanie, it's good you told me."

In the late afternoon Marjorie found her car wouldn't start. She went back inside and phoned the automobile club and the day-care centre. Then she waited, pacing, sitting, pacing, finally plopping herself down on the steps of the admitting wing to let the soft breezes soothe her troubled mind.

The young man who eventually arrived with tow truck and tools told her the ignition had been tampered with.

"Tampered?"

"You know, messed with."

"Why?"

"Someone trying to steal your car," he said. "Wasn't successful I guess."

"Why do you say that?"

"It's still here, ain't it?"

But by now Marjorie had noticed the empty salt packages and the greasy paper wrappers and she guessed correctly that her fuel tank would be nearly empty. On the way home it went around in her mind. Dromore and Melanie. Jeanie? No. No connection. Christ, what could she do? If she does something and Melanie's story turns out fiction she wouldn't be able to show her face. Even if it's true, even if all of it's true...She wished to hell she hadn't been so ready to listen, that Melanie hadn't told her. Christ. She needed to talk with somebody about it.

THIRTY-TWO

In the afternoon that he was given back his grounds privileges, Snow went looking for Hardy. At first he walked quietly and secretively in the woods but after twenty minutes of searching he realized he wouldn't be able to find him that way. He called then, in a controlled, projected voice and soon Matthew answered. Snow found him behind some heavy brush and a fallen fir tree. He had a lean-to half built and several blankets that Melanie must have smuggled to him. The boy's injuries appeared as bad in the day light as they had the night before but his eyes were clearer and less strain showed around his mouth.

"Did you get any sleep?"

"Yeah, Melanie brought me some blankets a few hours ago, but man it's sure wet around here."

"The rainy season's coming up."

"Yeah?"

"You can't last out here into October."

"I'll be gone by then, man." There was a tentative quality to his voice that Snow hadn't heard before.

"Sure. Anything I can help you with now?"

"Well, building this thing here maybe."

"Your lair."

"Lair?"

"That's what it's called." Snow gathered cedar boughs and lay them across the frame-work of saplings that Hardy had built against the fallen Douglas Fir. "Y'know you're not gonna make it out here, Matthew. C'mon back with me."

"No way, man. No fucking way."

"Okay. Look. I'll talk with Melanie. Anything specific you want?"

"Just toilet paper. I need some toilet paper."

When Snow left, Hardy was sitting on a rock in the sunlight staring into the forest. He'd give him a day or two, out of some strange sense of loyalty, but then if nobody could talk him in he'd better have a word with Brennan.

For a few days Snow passed the time pushing Karpov around the grounds, working with the outdoor crew and sneaking visits to Hardy. On the afternoon it rained, he stood beside Karpov at the window thinking of Hardy huddled in a blanket under the porous cover of his lean-to. A search of the ward had been conducted without turning up any female undergarments. The savant avoided Karpov and Snow. Snow was still waiting for his appointment with Pawlitsky.

"You worry too much, Robert. The boy is young; he will survive this."

"I don't think there's any way out for him, Victor. He's depressed now - he's convalescing - but when he gets the energy to move on and do something he'll probably go mad again."

"Why do you say that?"

"He's a manic depressive, Victor. Something they call a rapid cycler."

"Ahh. Dr. Snow's considered opinion."

"And Dr. Brennan."

"Hardy's not mad," said Karpov. "He merely lives in extremes. Madness is an invention of the withered, frightened little man who sits on a packet of coins by the fireplace. Madness is merely a possibility like anti-matter and black holes. We need the idea of madness in order to think well of our own actions."

Snow looked at him. "What about all these?" He gestured towards the men sitting, standing, talking, staring.

"Ah, there's the rub, Robert. The thought is not enough. It must be embodied, personified. So we select a few hapless souls and say that is madness, there it is."

"Right. But you have to admit Hardy needs help."

"That is true," said Karpov, and he sat silently for a moment. He seemed to have more trouble digesting the simple immediacy of Snow's statement than any number of abstract thoughts. "You must help him, Robert, as best you can. Here, I am out of matches. Wheel me over to our keeper."

Helping someone else, a novel idea. He hadn't had the inclination for what, two, three months. Early mornings were still shit but by mid-afternoon he found he could look beyond the turmoil in his own

162

frontal lobes. And Jennifer. She'd be there or she wouldn't be there when he got out of here. He could still live. "Victor, would it upset you greatly if I told you I'm gonna miss you, when I get out I mean?"

THIRTY-THREE

Hardy sat in the wet, drab, colorless woods, breathing slowly. He stared ahead unseeing. Above him whispered hemlock and firs, a voice in the distance, inaudible. For days now Melanie had come every afternoon and curled up beside him in the lean-to. It was the only time he felt warm. Snow brought what he could, including greetings from Karpov, and talked to him about coming back, back to the hospital, back home. He ate the tasteless food they delivered and defecated like an animal in the forest. All about him lay the spectacle of decay and growth, of death and rebirth. Rotting logs infested with ants and wood bugs, mildew, moulds, fungal growths, occasionally the transparent emerald green of a new seedling. On days that he could warm himself in the sun, pressing his back against a rock, he felt some hint of energy, some remnant from his past. He listened to the frogs at night, occasionally heard an owl, and wondered if a bear would wander by. He drank the water his friends brought him and washed his face in the moisture wrung from a cedar bough. As the air grew colder Hardy began to sense his power returning. He felt the spirit of the forest playing about his skin, entering his pores.

Snow noticed a change in Hardy. "He's beginning to look much better," he said to Melanie. To Karpov he said, "He's going high again."

When he visited Hardy, he often placed an arm around the boy's shoulder and pulled him close, a natural thing to do in the damp September air. Hardy let himself be held as naturally as he did anything else while Snow talked to him, tried to talk him into coming back. He tried to understand his rekindled feelings. He was friend, father, uncle to this boy. Occasionally the image from their washroom encounter entered Snow's brain but he saw it as a dream, some other life, something that had happened when he was dead.

He yearned for Jennifer still but made himself concentrate on the present, on himself, on others. He finally had his appointment with Pawlitsky. He told Pawlitsky he was ready to be discharged but as he talked he thought of all the things he would need to do, get some money from a bank account in Baltimore, contact the College and ask for a hearing, organize this and himself and fly to Baltimore to talk with Jennifer and as he talked his energy left him.

"You're still very depressed, Mr. Snow." said Pawlitsky.

"No. I'm much better."

"Do you have thoughts of harming yourself?"

"Not often now."

"What method would you chose?"

"What? I don't know. Pills."

"And do you hear voices?"

"No."

"Do you feel people are against you?"

"No."

"What about the medical director who caused you to lose your licence again?"

"He didn't like me."

"It was not your own failings?"

"Yes, some of it."

"But he was against you?"

"I thought so."

"Have you felt so bad that you thought you were bad?"

"I don't understand."

"Do you feel the need to be punished?"

"There was some of that. I think there was some of that."

"I will have the social worker talk to you about discharge, Mr. Snow."

"When?"

"She has a very big case load."

Snow let all this go by. He was still ambivalent. From in here where he was told what to do and when to do it, to the outside and all its confusion and decisions was a large step requiring energy and conviction.

Marjorie had not made a decision about Melanie and Dromore. She turned it over and over in her mind. She should write a letter to the College but each time she sat down to do it she was assailed by doubts and fears. Christ. To top it all off Melanie had not been avoiding Dromore as she had advised. She stayed for her appointments, continued to mutilate her forearms and went for long walks on the grounds in the afternoon. She felt sick thinking about it. And Jeanie was dead and forgotten. The newspapers weren't interested after the first report of a body being found on the grounds of the mental hospital. And the police were still looking for Hardy. She wondered where the hell he had gotten to.

She talked to Melanie again and tried to convince her to send a report to the complaints committee of the College, she'd help her write it, get the address and everything. Melanie merely shook her head, asked, "Can't you do anything, Dr. Brennan?"

Marjorie said, "Only if you'll testify, Mel. I have no proof, just what you've told me. Help me to help you."

Melanie walked away.

Each time Snow returned to the ward after his visits to Hardy, Karpov regaled him with small seminars on pantheism. Hardy was part of the forest now, an animal alive among animals, he said, one with the trees and insects, all part of God, and each one God. He envied Hardy, he told Snow, living as he was, off the land, feeling the cold, the sun, the rain and the hard rough earth. To Karpov, Hardy had returned to nature. "It is his natural state. The rest of us fight against it. The rest of us keep barriers between ourselves and nature. In the end the earth reclaims us anyway so it is all futile. Like Hardy we might as well cast away our clothes and run with deer and crawl with ants."

When Snow explained that Hardy wore clothes, slept in blankets and ate whatever food they could take to him, Karpov paid no attention. When he also told him that they had smuggled Hardy some toilet paper Karpov seemed genuinely disappointed.

Later, as was his style, Karpov reversed his philosophy. He told Snow that notions of natural man being better than, or morally superior to civilized man, were nonsense. "Besides," he said, "New York City and this institution are as natural as an ant hill. We have constructed both according to the laws of God and nature as they are programmed in the archives of our collective minds. Thoreau's Walden was a fake. The man got no closer to real nature, animal nature, than Tante Frieda gets to Europe on a ten day bus excursion. We are no better and no worse than savages. In fact, we are what we have been, we are what we are, and we are what we will become.

Hardy would do well to come in and get a hot meal and a change of clothes."

The news that Hardy was hiding in the woods above East Lawn crept slowly through the institution. The chronic men knew it first. As Snow had come to learn, they watched everything and always noticed a change in pattern. Perhaps they didn't know exactly what was happening, who was being hidden, but at times they seemed to read Snow's mind. They spoke to him of the coldness in the woods, of wild animals, of cowboys and Indians, and when he left one day with a bun under his coat, the idiot savant said, "I know what you're doing, I know what you're doing."

THIRTY-FOUR

Robert Snow was saying, "Look, there's something crazy going on. I gotta tell you before it's too late."

She'd been sitting in her office catching up on paperwork and trying to avoid thinking about the Dromore dilemma when he knocked on her door.

"Come in," she'd called, welcoming any distraction.

Snow had stuck his head in and said, "Can I talk with you a minute?"

She'd sat up and gestured him in.

Pushing papers to the side she said, "Go ahead."

He sat in the chair in front of her desk. "I know where Matthew Hardy is. It's embarrassing when I think about it."

"Where?"

"It's not that simple. I've been trying to get him to give himself up but he won't have anything to do with it."

"I don't understand."

"He was on the beach. That night we went out we brought him back."

"Wha'd'ya mean brought him back?"

"He's camped out in the woods, up above the buildings."

Marjorie looked at him. "You used my car."

"We...borrowed your car."

She was sitting up now, leaning forward. "You stole my car."

"Well, Melanie did, actually."

"Melanie?"

"She knows how to do it."

"Christ. I don't believe this. You stole my car, drove to some beach, picked up Hardy, and now he's camped in the woods somewhere."

"Bout sums it up."

"He's a fugitive."

"I know. I thought I could talk him into giving himself up."

"Well, I understand that kind of..."
"Pardon me?"
"Nothing. Forget it."
"The problem is he's going high again. He's been down and quiescent for awhile but now I think he's on his way up."
"Why are you telling me this?"
"I think it's time we did something, brought him in."
"Do you think he killed Jeanie?"
"He says he didn't."
"We could call the police and just tell them we've seen him on the grounds."
"I thought we could give it one more shot, to talk him in I mean. Maybe if you came. If that doesn't work we call the police."
"He won't listen to me."
"Maybe if we all go."
"All?"
"Me, Melanie, you, Victor Karpov."
"You think he'll come?"
"Worth one last try."
"Christ. When?"
"It's too late today. Tomorrow sometime."
"I don't know."
"I'll come and get you."
She sat back, "You're quite different."
"I feel different."
"No more depression?"
"Not as much."
"Still want to hide?"
Snow sighed, "I'm almost ready, to go back I mean."
"Try to get your licence reinstated, and this Jennifer person?"
"Yeah, I think so."
"Well, Dr. Snow, I hope it works out."
"I gotta talk Pawlitsky into discharging me first."
"If he won't, you could just walk. He won't send out an order."
"He might."
"That's true, he might."
"I'd like to see Hardy settled first."
"It's nice to see you caring a little."

"And that idiot savant. He's really demonic. How about giving his name to the police? Maybe they can find something."

"Because of the panties."

"I understand they never found Jeanie's."

"There's probably a dozen men in here who'd steal women's panties they get the chance."

"I imagine."

"And that's just counting staff."

Snow looked at her. She was gazing off somewhere, not smiling. Then she turned back to him, got up, leaned against the filing cabinet, and said, "Dr. Snow, there's something I need to talk about, as a colleague."

"As a colleague?"

"Yes."

"I'm a patient in here."

"I can't think of anyone else."

"Bottom of the line."

"Never mind. It doesn't matter."

"I'm sorry. Go ahead. I'm listening. I haven't been treated like a colleague for some time."

She sat down and told him Melanie's story. He muttered Christ almighty a couple of times but listened without otherwise interrupting. At the end he said, "Do you believe her?"

"I don't want to."

"But you do?"

"Yes."

"She won't write out a complaint?"

"No."

"So it's up to you."

"You've got it right."

"What's your greatest fear?"

"He's my boss, my supervisor. He's respected, he's brilliant..."

"And?"

"If it's all fantasy, or even if it's true and Melanie can't or won't prove it, I'm dead."

"Dead?"

"Well, not dead, lose my position, be too embarrassed to work again."

"Look, you report, they investigate."

"It's not that simple. He sues my ass."

"You could talk with him."

"What for? He's not gonna confess to me."

"Yeah, well, it's a tough one."

"But this kind of shit really burns me. Men abusing women I mean. Maybe he's doing it with others."

"So you feel compelled to do something?"

"Yes, goddamit, it makes me sick thinking about it. She's just a child."

"Well, you know, like a lot of things, it seems to boil down to courage."

"Courage?"

"Yeah, the courage to risk."

"Everything."

"Maybe not everything."

They sat silently for a minute. She looked him over closely. She was amazed how different he looked, how her perception had changed once she had placed him in a different category. "What would you do in the same situation?" she asked.

THIRTY-FIVE

Hardy sharpened the kitchen knife Melanie had brought him. As he fashioned it to a point against a rough piece of granite his energies focused, the glint of steel acting as a catalyst to coalesce the numbing diffusion in his mind. He felt his vision clear, his hearing improve. Once again his skin became sensitive to small breezes, a drop of water against his face, and the texture of his shirt against his body. He leaned his head back and inhaled the life of the forest - rich, thickly fresh, the smell of animals, fungus, mould. His body grew back to its full six-one and the muscles in his arms throbbed to life. He began to feel that something marvellous was about to happen, something big. And he, Mat Hardy, would be the centre of it all.

His heart grew in his chest all day and night. His legs and arms ached for action. He moved. He leapt from deadfall to deadfall, stopped and rubbed against the massive trees,
climbed high in a giant cedar, drank from a small brook and listened to the wolves passing messages around him, about him. He knew the animals would gather, the people would gather. They'd come to hear him speak.

For a time, from the edge of the forest in the darkness, he looked down on the buildings of Essondale, watching their amber windows. When he returned to his lean-to he was visited by a snowy white Arctic Owl. It landed in a branch above Hardy's head with barely a sound. At first he saw it only through the reflection of moonlight in its eyes, and then, as his vision grew accustomed to the darkness and the distance, he saw the whiteness of its feathers and the quick tilting of its head. It listened carefully when Hardy asked, "What d'ya want from me, owl? Wha' do I do next?"

When the owl replied, Hardy felt its breath against his skin, its voice inside his ears, its feathers across his eyes. The sound was low and painful and shook the trees and rocks. He felt as if his whole body were a single sensory organ attuned to the owl so that its call might reach to the lower vaults of his mind and turn a key.

As suddenly as it had appeared, the bird was gone, but Hardy went with him. He left his body sitting on the rock and flew in the snow white feathers of the owl, through the dark forest, over the tips of conifers, past the shadow of the moon to the barren ice fields of the Rocky Mountains. He sat in his own skin watching the owl circle above and he looked down upon himself from high over the forest where the air was thin and cold.

It rained all morning. Pushed by Pacific Westerlies, heavy charcoal clouds moved across Vancouver and up the Fraser Valley. Marjorie looked out her kitchen window and thought how cold, dark and dreary the institution would be on a day like this. She remembered her promise to Snow and, like many of her decisions, she knew she would live to regret it. She had agreed to go with him at two in the afternoon to visit Hardy in the woods and try to talk him back in. If they failed she would return and notify the police.

Still, she hoped the problem (and the weather) would resolve itself by the time she met Snow.

With John at the hospital, she felt quite alone that morning. Mechanically she got Adam dressed, fed, slickered up, extra socks, giving herself only a cursory glance in the mirror. She sat for a few minutes with a hot coffee mug clenched in both hands, absentmindedly talking with Adam, what, Honey, mommy coming, just a minute sweetie, then gathered her purse, her keys, her raincoat, the green fold up umbrella, Adam's rain hat, and left the apartment shivering against the late September dampness with her son in tow.

Between the day-care and Essondale, Marjorie cursed the rain and her own lack of power, conviction. The defrost worked poorly despite a trip to the dealer last week. A man would have gotten better service. The weather, the institution, her patients, her marriage, car mechanics, Snow, Hardy, Melanie, Dromore...nothing she felt she could influence, let alone control. As a woman she was impotent, as a customer she was impotent, as a physician she was impotent, as a healer she was impotent. She could walk through her part or not; it made no difference. Mechanics remained incompetent, husbands inattentive, institutions puerile, patients crazy, some men abusive, maybe even murderous. I, Marjorie Brennan, can do nothing for anybody. She said it out loud, first softly, and then she repeated the phrase in a sort of Gregorian chant. To her surprise she found the experience pleasing. It eased the tension building in her forehead from squinting through the condensation on her windscreen.

She tried a few more self-derogatory phrases and settled on a string of profanity, finding some now archaic words from her childhood.

As she drove through the gates of Essondale she felt better and began to think about the nature of healing. Maybe the acceptance of her powerlessness would make her a stronger healer. Or maybe it's all bullshit. She just needed to take hold of things, for a change.

She pulled into a parking spot and waited for a few minutes for a lessening of the insistent rain against her windows. At any rate something might come from admitting her impotence, her insecurity. Besides, Robert Snow is better isn't he? One out of ten's not so bad.

Through the morning she spent long periods of time warming her hands over the radiator in the nursing station, looking out at the ward and then through the high windows into the slashing rain and beyond. Melanie hovered near the station, asking of inconsequential matters, appearing like she wanted to say something to Marjorie but never managing to find the words. She hovered like a bad conscience. Marjorie didn't ask her anything. What more could Melanie tell her that would make the situation any better? She'd have to make a decision soon if she wanted to live with herself. She wished it would go away but knew it wouldn't.

Over lunch Marjorie was preoccupied. She kept glancing out the window at the steady downpour. She accepted a coffee from Dromore without thinking and then felt embarrassed, guilty, angry, confused. She was sure she was blushing. She excused herself, told him she had an appointment. Through the window she could see the rain ease and then stop. It was replaced by an eerie pre-dawn light. A lull in the storm. She sought the solitude of her office and once there sat, her feet resting on the coffee table, her mind embraced by the tiny room and its familiar trappings. Her umbrella lay tangled and useless on the office floor, her raincoat, still damp, hanging on the back of the door. Involuntarily she shivered, wrapped her arms around herself and settled deep into her chair to await the rendezvous with Snow.

It was one-thirty when Snow wheeled Karpov to the door. The orderly looked up, said, "Not today, fellas."

"What?"

"Pawlitsky took away your grounds privileges."

"What?"

"Confined to ward."

"For Christ's sake."

"You should watch your language, Robert."

Karpov muttered, "Fascist pig."

Snow wheeled him away. "Take it easy Victor. You still have your key?"

"Yes."

"I'll create a diversion."

Snow wandered into the washroom. He took a roll of toilet paper and stuffed it into a toilet. Then he reached into the tank, pulled the stopper and bent the float. The toilet bowl filled quickly and began to overflow. He walked back into the dayroom-dormitory and said to the orderly, "There's a toilet in there flooding."

Reluctantly the orderly got up and went to look.

Snow moved quickly. With Karpov's key he unlocked the door, pushed the wheelchair out, followed without looking back and shut the door behind himself. "Once again across the barren wastes of Siberia," said Karpov. "The Gulag behind, Moscow awaits."

"We'll use the elevator this time."

He pushed Karpov down the corridor to the iron grilled elevator and leaned on the wall button. It was an old Otis and it missed the landing by three inches when it rumbled up from the basement. Snow pulled the grill open and then the door, helped Karpov in, let the doors swing shut and then pushed button number one. Nothing happened.

"There is an irony here that pleases me," said Karpov, but Snow pulled the doors tighter and pushed the button again. This time the mechanism jerked to life and lowered the two escapees to the ground floor.

Once outside, Snow stopped for a moment to tuck Karpov's blanket around his legs and to pull his own collar up around his neck. The rain had stopped but the skies told him this was a temporary reprieve. Halfway down the hill Dr. Brennan was standing in the shelter of the Tuck shop waiting for them, her arms folded tightly across her slate grey Mackintosh. As Snow and Karpov approached from above, Melanie came up the walk from below. She had a yellow rain slicker pulled over a thick woollen sweater.

"I'm coming with you," she announced, when she reached Marjorie.

Marjorie turned to the two coming from West Lawn. "Hello, Mr. Karpov. How are you making out?"

Snow said, "We'll leave him at the edge of the woods."

"Once again," said Karpov, "a collection of fools embark on a strange odyssey."

"You wanted to come, Victor."

"I do. I do. Hardy must be saved. He carries the soul of each and every one of us. We are all doomed to lives of order and predictability without Hardy. He carries our courage. Besides, ..."

"Besides what?" said Snow, turning Karpov's wheelchair. "I...like him."

"We better hurry," said Brennan. "Its gonna start again. Lead the way, Dr. Snow."

Snow waited for Karpov to light a new cigarette and then, pushing the wheelchair, he led Marjorie and Melanie up the hill. They passed Westlawn, continuing upwards until they came to the edge of the forest. Fresh streams had broken pathways in the grass and their feet were quickly soaked. The soft ground made difficult passage for the wheelchair and Snow was breathing heavily by the time he reached the first trees. Pausing to rest, he turned back and surveyed the grounds of Essondale below him. The buildings seemed etched in unusual clarity by the white September light penetrating the damp air. A new bank of black cumulous clouds rose above the horizon to the west. The wind chilled his fingers and ears and he thought how wet and cold Hardy must be. Far down at the base of the admitting wing some movement caught his eye. He looked more intently and saw a group of people gathering outside the back door of the clinic.

"Okay. We better get moving. Victor, you'll have to stay here." He pushed the wheelchair under a large cedar tree. "Hardy's two hundred yards or so that way." He pointed northwest into the dense forest.

Melanie took the lead now, scrambling around bushes, over rocks, across deadfalls. Snow stayed behind and helped Marjorie pick her way through the undergrowth. The wet foliage shook its water on Snow and his sweater hung limply around his hips. The clouds began to gather overhead and, occasionally broken by brief shafts of light, a false dusk descended. Marjorie stumbled, felt her knee scrape the ground and tear her pantyhose. He took her arm, helped her up and pulled her along the route he had used several times before. Melanie disappeared ahead.

It began to rain again, intermittently at first and then with a steady rhythm. Snow helped Marjorie over a fallen log and when she was down and facing him he stopped to look at her, still holding her arm. Her hair was flattened wet and falling over her eyes. She pushed it back with her free hand and looked at Snow standing there, sodden. Cold water ran down her face, down her neck, but her eyes sparkled with life. She smiled, said, "You know this is ridiculous."

He had an urge to kiss her and for a moment he almost did, and she, reading his thoughts, quickly walked ahead. Snow smiled then, and Marjorie looked back and smiled with him. He caught up to her and took her arm again.

They heard Melanie calling before they reached Hardy's lair and when they got there she told them he was gone. "I've looked all around. He's not here. But his pants are over there, in a pile, with some sweaters and shirts."

"Does he have other clothes?" asked Marjorie.

"Just one pair of pants is all. He's taken his clothes off."

Snow could hear thunder in the distance. "Christ. He'll die of exposure out here." He shouted: "Hardy. Matthew Hardy."

"I don't see his boots anywhere," said Marjorie.

"He would never leave his boots."

"Come on, we'll have to look for him."

As they turned away from the lean-to they heard a faint cry through the rain in the trees.

"What the hell was that?"

"Was it Matthew?"

"No. It sounded like Karpov."

They heard it again, more distinctly this time, Karpov shouting, "ROBERT." His voice was followed by a clap of thunder.

"We better go back and see what he wants."

Snow led the way on their return journey, with Melanie lagging behind, making side excursions into the bush to call for Hardy. When they reached the edge of the forest they were drenched and hurting. Snow had torn his sweater and Marjorie had green stains and mud smeared on her raincoat. Karpov was sitting where they had left him. Snow let his gaze follow Karpov's. The Bulgarian was staring up the hill in the direction of a podium-like knoll lying at the forest edge, high above the sprawling Essondale estate. On top of the knoll stood Hardy, naked but for his tooled leather boots. His feet were planted wide apart, his body glistened in the rain, his eyes were black and deep and knowing. He held his right hand high with the sharpened kitchen knife pointing skyward. From Snow's vantage point, Hardy appeared to stand seven, eight feet tall. And in front of him, as if a separate being, a living thing, a wilful taunting animal, proud and defiant in its nakedness, rose Hardy's pole, his sword, his cock.

"It's enormous," whispered Karpov.

To Snow and Marjorie it looked big as well but Snow was sure the illusion had something to do with perspective.

Snow brushed rain from his eyes and looked away from Hardy, down the hill. Thunder was rumbling in the distance and jagged lightning flared briefly in the sky. Far below people seemed to be walking up the hill, some in white. They were coming from Essondale's buildings and they were looking at Hardy. Beyond the buildings he could see two police cars pulling into the parking lot, their red lights revolving, sparkling, diffracting in the rain. He turned back to Hardy. The cowboy was talking in a loud and resonating voice.

"They have come to listen," he said. "I knew they would come to listen."

"Matthew. For God's sake put that knife down."

Karpov rolled his chair closer to the foot of Hardy's knoll. Melanie emerged from the forest and ran to Hardy, and knelt at his feet. Hardy kept his head up, his eyes glaring straight ahead. He waved the knife in a circle and intoned, "Me alone, all alone. I stand here alone. Against the whole fucking universe. Fuck my father. Fuck the teachers. Fuck the police. Fuck Essondale. You can't get Mat Hardy no more. Mat Hardy's bigger'n all of you."

"He's psychotic again," said Marjorie.

"He's having a transcendental experience," said Karpov.

"Take me with you," said Melanie.

"Hardy, come down off that hill so we can help you," shouted Snow. "Give me the knife. The police are coming. I don't wanna see you get hurt."

His last words were lost in a roll of thunder.

"I'm free now," said Hardy. "Free of all of you. You can't get me now. Me and the owl. The owl is my brother. I drink rain and breathe the wind. I control the thunder and lightning."

Marjorie took a few steps closer. "You have power now, Matthew. Nobody can hurt you now. You don't need the knife anymore. Come and get some clothes on. You must be cold." She had trouble keeping her eyes off his impressive erection.

"I'm not cold," said Hardy. "I don't feel cold no more."

"That's good," said Marjorie. "That's fine. Just come down. Walk with us. That's all. Show us where you're going. Let us help you, Matthew."

Snow could recognize some faces in the crowd walking slowly up the hill. Dromore and Pawlitsky, the idiot savant, Bessie.

"I don't need no help. You're the ones who don't know nothing. You're the ones who need help. You're the sick ones, the wackos, the psychos. And I have the power to let you know, to let you know...about immortality."

"Christ, he almost sounds like you, Victor."

"I am you," said Hardy. "And you, and you, and you." He swept the hillside with his knife. "But I'm bigger'n all you together."

"You're right, Matthew. You're right." Marjorie moved closer still. "You're strong, very strong. You don't have to be afraid any longer. We won't take over your mind. We couldn't do that. Come and talk with me, Matthew. I'm the one afraid now. Come and help me."

Hardy looked down at Brennan now, standing before him, shivering, water dripping down her face, eyes wide, pleading with him. "I'm okay, Doc. Really I am."

"Then come down, Matthew. Come down with me. Help me back."

Hardy's knife hand dropped to his side. He looked directly at Brennan, then Snow, Karpov, and Melanie at his feet. Snow took a step forward. Brennan almost had him. Poor bastard, challenging the world to do its worst. And Snow knew it would. Now or later. And the more bravado in Hardy's voice, the more Snow sensed loneliness and fear. Hardy was making a grand and futile gesture, the kind of action that elevated man above the animals but always failed to reach the height of angels.

"The trouble with western intellectual thought," Karpov was saying, "is that it doesn't permit the notion of alternative realities. Perhaps Hardy has left us for another sphere."

"For Christ's sake, shut up, Victor," said Snow, and then to Hardy. "You know you can trust us, Matthew. Come with Dr. Brennan. Your mind is your own. Your thoughts are your own. Your soul too. Dr. Brennan's right."

Hardy was wavering. His body sagged a little, his erection drooped, the knife dangled loosely in his hand.

"Dr. Snow is right," said Karpov. "And Dr. Brennan too."

He pushed his chair through the mud and rain to the foot of the knoll.

Hardy was close to letting go. Close to giving in. Just another minute, maybe two, and he'd come down, he'd collapse, he'd cry.

But at that moment the wind carried the voice of Dr. Dromore up the hill to Hardy's ears. "Anybody brought some Haldol we can give him?"

Hardy straightened out like a bear smelling danger. His knife hand thrust above his head.

"Haldol!" he shouted. "Chlorpromazine! Lithium! Bubble rooms! Orders! Shock treatment! Fuck'em all. You've had my body. You want it again, and my mind as well. You can't fucking touch me!" He was screaming now, eyes upward, screaming at the sky, rain beating on his face, arm thrust high, face twisted, tortured, every muscle in his body taut. Howling like a wolf. "OOOOOOOwwwwwwooo."

"No, Matthew, no. Don't do it. Come down. We won't hurt you."

"I want life," he screamed at the clouds, as more lightning lit up his face and froze the crowd.

But they were coming now, with Dromore giving orders to reluctant nurses, the police lower down, coming up the hill.

"Give him some room," shouted Snow. "Give him some space." But it was too late.

A white coat moved in quickly to tackle Hardy from behind. Hardy sprang over Melanie, bounded past Karpov, Karpov muttering rapidly. The white coat lunged at Hardy and hit Karpov. The Bulgarian's chair tipped over backward in the mud.

Hardy raced past Marjorie, past Snow. Both shouted after him.

The crowd scattered, and taking huge steps, rising high above the ground, Hardy's body, glistening naked, galloped down the hill.

From below, Snow thought later, it must have been a frightening sight. With thunder rumbling, the skies flashing in anger or fear, this huge animal bounding straight down, straight down at you, a knife held high in strike position, looking like nothing could stop it, like nothing could get out of the way, in the cold rain, the slippery mud, and the scream. Hardy's scream. A piercing, painful, bone chilling scream, like someone falling off a building.

Straight through the patients, through the nurses scattering, straight toward two police officers. One moved aside but the other froze on the spot and drew his gun. There was shouting through the screaming, Hardy barrelling down, flying down, the knife above his head. The cop stood firm under the dark sky, the buildings of a lunatic asylum at his back, brooding over his shoulder, the rain in his eyes, Hardy closing on him fast. He drew his gun and shot Hardy point blank.

Snow heard the shot, felt it like a needle in his chest, watched Hardy keep moving, watched him still flying down the hill. But now he'd snared the cop and the two were flying down, crashing, rolling down, over and over. Snow saw it in slow motion, the bodies tumbling and finally coming to rest at the back of the Tuck Shop. Then he was running, running down the hill, and Brennan was running after him, slipping, falling, picking herself up.

They got there just before the others. The cop was sitting up, dazed, blood on his uniform. Hardy was sprawled awkwardly, face in the mud, the knife still in his outstretched hand, his boots gone. Snow quickly rolled him over and saw the hole in the centre of his chest, his open mouth, the muddied eyes. Marjorie knelt beside him and felt for a pulse in his neck. Snow listened to his chest, then thumped his chest, then put the heels of his palms on Hardy's sternum and pumped.

Blood spurted from the wound. Marjorie stood up slowly, looked at Snow, knelt again and checked the cop. The blood seemed to be Hardy's. He had no visible injuries. She stood again, leaning against the back of the Tuck Shop. She said, "It's too late, Robert."

The others, who had paused to watch them, moved in now. Dromore shouted instructions, for stretchers, ambulance. Snow stood up but Pawlitsky got down on his knees and pounded on Hardy's chest, spraying more blood around. Someone else was bent over him, blowing air into his lungs.

Snow knew it wouldn't work. Hardy was gone, his heart ruptured by the bullet.

Melanie stood quietly at the edge of the circle, staring at the scene. Dromore tried to shoo the crowd of patients away. Marjorie walked over and took Melanie in her arms. The child sobbed on her breast, shuddering. Marjorie held her tightly, and looked up into the rain.

Snow remembered Karpov and walked away from the crowd, pulled himself back up the hill. When he got back to the knoll he found Karpov's chair flipped over backward, the poet's head in the mud, his useless feet in the air.

Karpov was cursing and muttering, "Jesus, God Almighty. Jesus. Remove me from here. What's happened?"

Snow pulled him out of the mud and righted his chair.

"Where's Matthew? What's happening?"

"Hardy's been shot."

"Shot? By a bullet?"

"He's dead, Victor. I think he's dead."

"Dead? Not Matthew?"

"He was running down. A cop shot him."

"No. Not the police. The gods. He must have angered the gods."

"Maybe. Either way we can't help him now."

"He's down there? In that crowd?"

"Yes."

"He hates crowds, Robert." And then Karpov shouted into the rain, "Get away from him, desecrators, blasphemers."

They watched from the hill as a stretcher appeared and Hardy's body was rolled onto it and carried toward the buildings. The cop was helped away. The crowd began to disperse. Melanie and Marjorie still stood in the rain, clinging to one another.

Snow took his place behind Karpov's chair and slowly wheeled him down the slippery hill. He began to feel the rain, soaked through all his clothes, squishing coldly. Karpov was watching the ambulance disappear around the side of the first building. He said something in a language Snow didn't know, and then, "You see, Robert, you see. There is no place in this world for a freedom loving man. Even the gods are threatened."

"It was an accident, Victor."

"I know," said Karpov. "I know." And Snow imagined that the cripple's mind had drifted to the accident that ruined his own body years before. A tear ran down Karpov's face. "I hated him, Robert," he said. "I hated his muscles, his flesh, his youth, his body."

"You loved him as well," said Snow.

"Yes, Robert, I loved him...also."

When they reached the two women, Marjorie pulled Melanie along and the four moved slowly toward the buildings.

"I'm leaving tonight," Snow said to Marjorie.

"Good. You should do that. I'm glad."

Snow turned back to Karpov's head. "Victor, I want you to come with me."

Karpov looked at the clouds. "The rain's easing. It will break very soon."

"Did you hear me?"

"I heard you, Robert." He lowered his gaze back to the buildings.

"I'll find a place for you in Vancouver."

"You want me to live with you, Robert?"

"Until I get myself sorted out, and you settled."

"A week, a month?"

Snow held back on the chair and all four paused. "I don't know, Victor. We'll have to see."

"Will you lift me in and out of the bath, Robert? Will you wash out the bottles I piss in? Will you keep me clean and dusted? Will you wipe my ass? Will you disimpact me when I need it?"

Snow looked off in the distance. "For a while, until we get nursing and home care organized."

"I'm not ready, Robert."

"I can't stay one day longer, Victor. I have to go now."

"You go then, Robert. I'll come later, maybe a month or two..."

"I can't wait for you."

"I know, Robert. I know."

"You silly bastard. You've gotta get outa here."

"It's not so easy."

"D'y'wanna live in Westlawn the rest of your life?"

"I don't live in Westlawn, Robert."

Snow said, "You can dream just as well in the city."

"Take me back to the ward, Robert. I must mourn Matthew in my own way."

"One day they'll discharge you anyway, Mr. Karpov," said Marjorie.

"Perhaps." He was fussing and searching around his chair. "I can't find my cigarette papers."

Snow said, "We'll get you some."

It had stopped raining. They paused outside the back door of the admitting wing, as if reluctant to go their separate ways. Marjorie was saying, "We all need to get dry. A nurse can take Victor back to Westlawn."

Karpov had found a paper and was rolling a cigarette from his pouch of tobacco.

Snow looked at Marjorie still holding Melanie close to her, then at Karpov. He knew he had to leave them, say goodbye, walk away, wet or dry. He had to do it now.

Marjorie said, "Maybe we can get you some dry clothing on West 3. They always have some."

The back door of the admitting wing opened and Dromore stepped out. He scanned the four of them briefly. "Dr. Brennan, I'll take Melanie now. You go get yourself dried off."

Marjorie stared at him, and then looked at Snow.

Dromore said, "Come along, Melanie."

Marjorie held onto Melanie's arm. She said, "Professor Dromore, I'd like to talk with you first."

"After I see Melanie, Dr. Brennan, and you've cleaned yourself up."

"No. I'll talk with you now."

Dromore looked at the four of them. He said, "Very well," and turned to enter the admitting wing.

Snow said, "Good luck."

"You too."

He watched her back as she followed Dromore. Melanie watched too, and then said, "I'll take Victor back to Westlawn."

Karpov, searching for a match, was saying, "The path is marked only by obstacles. Avoid them and you lose your way."

Snow said, "I'll walk with you." He helped Melanie push the chair up the slope in the direction of Westlawn.

Karpov had given up his search for matches. Without looking at Snow he said, "Are you going back to Baltimore, Robert?"

Snow said, "Yeah, one way or another."

When they reached Westlawn they pulled Karpov's chair backwards up the steps to the main entrance. Inside the building Snow touched Melanie's cheek and said, "You do whatever Dr. Brennan asks you, okay? She'll really help you if you let her."

Melanie nodded.

Snow bent over to give the old poet a hug, but Karpov, looking tired, wet, and forlorn, turned his head away and began to talk of Thomas Mann.

THIRTY-SIX

On a warm, windy day in April the following year, Victor Karpov sat in his wheelchair high on the hill above the buildings of Essondale, a tartan blanket wrapped around his legs. A letter from Dr. Robert Snow lay in his lap as he looked down on Eastlawn and Westlawn and the few people out walking the grounds. He rolled himself a cigarette, hunching in his chair to prevent the wind from blowing his makings away. When the cigarette was lit to his satisfaction he read Snow's letter again.

> Dear Victor,
> I hope this letter reaches you in or out of Essondale, and finds you in good health and good spirits. I think of you often. I have been sober now for nine months. They took me back at the hospital with a limited licence & I have a hearing coming up in June. This time I'll make it. I'm busy most evenings taking refresher courses at Hopkins, sitting in on clinics & the other evenings I see Jennifer, the lady I talked about. She - well, you don't need to hear about it, but I think we're going to make it. I have to admit it, Victor, I feel really good. Of course I haven't heard anything about Essondale & Drs. Brennan & Dromore & you & Melanie. I'd like you to write to me. Once I know my letter got to you I'll send you a longer one.

Karpov decided he'd write, yes he'd write Robert Snow a letter, and tell him Brennan had left to work in a downtown hospital, Dromore was still here but there were rumours of other women coming forward, and Hardy's body had been shipped back to Alberta with the cops saying the investigation into Jeanie's death is still open but not doing anything, and the idiot savant still doing his dates and bragging about the person he killed, and Melanie, Brennan discharging her last September but getting readmitted only a couple of weeks ago.

He felt pleased for Robert Snow, but to himself he murmured, "Illusion, all illusion." He looked up at the forest where Hardy had hidden. His eyes fixed on a splash of white high in the trees. A sudden gust of wind swept Snow's letter off his lap as he watched the show-white owl stretch its wings, blink its eyes, tilt its head as if about to speak, and then settle back, blind, waiting. He rolled his chair along and made a futile grab at the letter that had now caught an updraft and was spiralling across the hill. When he looked back the owl was gone.

Two figures approached him on the blacktop path. One was a young doctor in tweed jacket, sucking on a pipe, hands in his pockets, walking on the up side of the sloping sidewalk. The other was Melanie. Back again. She was wearing jeans and a bulky wool sweater. She appeared sweet, innocent, perhaps sixteen. As she walked beside the new doctor she looked up at him with big round curious eyes.

When they passed in front of Karpov he could hear their conversation. The young man was saying, "It's like we talked about, Melanie, you do this projective identification thing. You're not really sure where you end and other people begin. It's like you put parts of yourself into other people."

"Totally brilliant," said Melanie. "My father used to come on to me when I was real young."

"Well, sexual abuse is very common in women with your kind of problem. The cathexis of an ambiguous love object."

"Yeah," said Melanie. "Awesome. I understand now. Nobody ever explained it to me before. Not this way. I really feel I can talk with you, Dr. Taynen. You see things so clearly."

Karpov watched them pass to his left, their voices dying quickly on the breeze. Then taking a deep drag on his cigarette he surveyed his world of lunatics, charlatans, seekers and spoilers, the innocent and the not so innocent. He looked longingly at the clouding sky. Then he let the brake off his silver chariot, and, with a long, low chuckle that sang with the wind in the trees, rolled rapidly down the hill.

Printed in the United States
136006LV00001B/29/P